The **REVELATION** of

JESUS CHRIST

REVEALED

By, Freddie L. Butler

Publisher: Stanton Publishing House
Library of Congress Registration Number: 2018913981
ISBN-13: 9781987011012 (BARNES & NOBLES)
ISBN-13: 9781790254859 (KDP AMAZON)
Printed in the United States of America
Cover & Interior Design by Stanton Publishing House

TO: SISTER PAM,
MY SISTER IN THE LORD.
GOD'S BEST TO YOU AND
YOUR FAMILY !! !

T.J. Butler
05/20/2019

DEDICATION

When I look back over my life, without a doubt, I know that I owe my life and any success in this life to my Lord and Savior Jesus Christ. It is Jesus who has kept me safe in a career in law enforcement where so many have given their lives for. It is Jesus who brought me into contact with all the good people who have positively influenced me along the way. I give Jesus all the credit and glory for this book!

INTRODUCTION

The author, Freddie L. Butler Jr., an ordained minister, has by the help of almighty God prayerfully attempted to explain each chapter by verse in the book of Revelation. This quest began in a small country church with a class that my Pastor authorized called the "Believer's Class." During the very first class in September 2013, those attending requested that the subject taught and discussed in this class be the book of Revelation.

It took two years to write and teach the content of this book, The Revelation of Jesus Christ Revealed.

The first five words of Revelation in your bible are actually the title (Revelation 1:1). The book of Revelation contains events that have been concealed but are now revealed through this book in the bible.

My prayer is that as you read your bible the book of Revelation will no longer be the book in the bible to be avoided, but instead will be the book that peak your interest. As you study the book of Revelation in your bible you must keep in mind the scripture found in 2 Peter 3:8. The book of Revelation in your bible records more than a thousand years of events but thank God the Church will not experience any of it!

This book you are holding was not meant to stand alone but instead is provided to assist you in your study time and prayerfully will lead you into and through the book of Revelation. You will find a number of scriptures referenced like the one in 2 Peter, but not written out in this book. Therefore, you will need your bible during these times. So take your time and enjoy your study time with God!!! Maybe it won't take you two years as it did me.

Be blessed and thank you for your prayers.

CHAPTER 1

Revelation 1:1, Read

The first five words of this book are actually the title. The word translated *Revelation (Apokalypsis, uh-pock-uh-lip-sis)* is the word from which we get the English word "apocalypse." It means "an uncovering" or "to reveal." The Book of Revelation contains events that have been concealed but are now revealed.

As we study this book, we must keep in mind 2 Peter 3:8 (Read). You will find as we study that, this book records more than a thousand years of events.

10

According to Revelation 1:1, God gave this revelation to Jesus Christ to show unto his servant's things which must shortly come to pass, and he sent and signified it by his angel unto his servant John. This makes Jesus the author of this book, even though John is the human writer.

It is believed that John wrote the Book of Revelation around 93 A.D. from the island of Patmos, an island off the coast of present-day Turkey. John was banished to Patmos by the Roman Emperor Domitian who ruled 81–96 A.D. Domitian was the first Roman Emperor to enforce worship of the Roman Emperor. Once a year, every Roman citizen was required to confess "Caesar is Lord," but Christians refused. The Book of Revelation can be outlined in five sections:

1. Revelation Chapters 1–3, the church age.

2. Revelation Chapters 4–5, events in heaven.

3. Revelation Chapters 6–19, events of the future tribulation.

4. Revelation Chapter 20, events of the millennium.

5. Revelation Chapters 21–22, events of new heavens and new earth.

The Church Age (current times)

Revelation 1:3, Read

Three groups of people are blessed:

1. Those who read The Revelation

2. Those who hear it

3. Those who keep the things written in this book

We will humbly make an attempt, by the grace of God and the presence of the Holy Spirit, to study and understand this book that is so often avoided and feared.

Revelation 1:4, Read

The number 7 depicts completeness. There are a number of times where the number 7 is used throughout the Book of Revelation.

Another example is found in Revelation 5:6, Read.

We know that there is but one Holy Spirit as stated in Ephesians 4:4–6. So, *Revelation 5:6* is not suggesting that there are actually Seven Spirits of God. Let's see how it is explained in the book of Isaiah.

Isaiah 11:2, Read

There are seven titles given to the Holy Spirit:

1. The Spirit of the Lord

2. Wisdom

3. Understanding

4. Counsel

5. Might

6. Knowledge

7. The fear of the Lord (or reverence)

Revelation 1:4–6, Read

The Holy Trinity is represented in these verses:

1. Verse 4 the Holy Spirit.

2. Verse 5 Jesus Christ our savior.

3. Verse 6 God the Father.

Here, we have the Holy Trinity represented in the final book of the bible and in the first book, Genesis, in the first three verses.

Genesis 1:1–3, Read

1. Verse 1 God the Father.

2. Verse 2 the Spirit of God/Holy Spirit.

3. Verse 3 the Word of God, Jesus (John 1:14).

It is important that we understand that in the Book of Revelation, there is the *Holy Trinity* and later there will be the *unholy trinity.*

Revelation 1:11, Read

Jesus commissions John to write the Book of Revelations and to send it to the seven churches. As was stated earlier, the number 7 represents completeness. There were other churches at the time, for example, the churches of *Corinth and Colossian.* So, I believe the Lord chose these seven churches because they represent present-day churches and Christians as a whole.

Revelation 1:12–16, Read

Jesus is talking to John in verse 11. In the verses, we just Read John *turned to see the voice that spoke* and he describes what he sees. Notice John describes the Lord's head, hair, eyes, and voice which suggest John was looking toward the face. However, John does not describe the face of the Lord because he did not see the Lord's face, which validates the truth found in 1 Timothy 6:16, Read.

Revelation 1:17–18

Keys of hell and of death signify power and authority.

Revelation 1:19

Here, John is told to write:

1. *The things thou hast seen,* that is the vision of Christ in the midst of the candlesticks (Rev 1).

2. *The things which are,* that is, the things concerning the churches, which John wrote in Revelation Chapters 2–3.

3. *The things which shall be hereafter,* that is events which MUST BE after the churches (Rev 4:1–22:5).

We are currently in *the things which are,* the church age.

Revelation 1:20, Read

Here, Jesus explains and interprets to John what he has seen in verses 12–16. The seven stars are the angels or pastors of the seven churches. The seven candlesticks are the seven churches.

CHAPTER 2

Revelation 2:1–7

This is the epistle to the church of Ephesus. This is where we get the book of Ephesians in our New Testament bibles. Some facts about the church of Ephesus are:

1. There are 10 points of commendations mentioned (v 2–6).

2. There is one point of condemnation (v 4–5).

3. They had left their first love (v 4).

4. They were commanded to repent and do their first works to be restored to God and their first love (v 5).

5. If they would not do so, they would be removed (v 5).

6. The whole church would be destroyed if the terms were not met (v 5). This would also be true of individuals because we are the church.

7. Only the overcomer was promised heaven (v 7).

Revelation 2:8–11

This is the epistle to the church of Smyrna. Remember the angel of the church is the pastor. Three things were commended of Smyrna:

1. Works

2. Tribulation

3. Poverty but rich in the Lord

Smyrna was one of the seven churches not condemned by the Lord.

Revelation 2:12–17

This is the epistle to the church of Pergamos. Three things were commended of Pergamos:

1. Works (v 13)

2. Holding fast to Christ name (v 13)

3. Not denying the faith (v 13)

Four things were condemned in Pergamos (v 14–15):

1. Holding the doctrine of Balaam

2. Eating things sacrificed to idols

3. Committing fornication

4. Holding the doctrine of Nicolaitans

To understand the *doctrine of Balaam,* you need to go back to Numbers 22 to understand the stumbling block it created for the believers. When Reading those passages, remember that Balaam was a priest; if you Read far enough, you will find where Balaam's donkey spoke to him.

The *Nicolaitans* were a group who practiced and taught immoral doctrines like having community wives was acceptable and that committing adultery and fornication was not sinful. They also believed that eating meals offered to idols was lawful.

Revelation 2:18–29

This is the epistle to the church of Thyatira. Six things were commending Thyatira:

1. Works

2. Charity

3. Service

4. Faith

5. Patience

6. Increased works

Four things were against Thyatira:

1. Permitting Jezebel to teach

2. Permitting her to seduce Christians to commit fornication

3. Permitting her to seduce Christians to eat things sacrificed

to idols

4. Tolerating her in spite impenitence (failure to repent)

CHAPTER 3

Revelation 3:1–6

This is the epistle to the church of Sardis. Four things were about Sardis:

1. Works

2. Having a name or reputation of being alive church, but "art dead."

3. Works not perfect before God (v 2)

4. Few godly members (v 4)

Five commands to Sardis:

1. Be watchful (v 2)

2. Strengthen the things that remain

3. Remember your teaching (v 3)

4. Hold fast (v 3)

5. Repent (v 3)

Revelation 3:7–13

This is the epistle to the church of Philadelphia. The church of Philadelphia is the second of the seven churches that were not condemned. Remember the church of Smyrna was the other one.

However, Jesus does have 10 predictions for the church of Philadelphia:

1. I will expose all liars.

2. I will humble them before you.

3. I will confirm my love for you to them.

4. I will keep you from persecution (v 10).

5. I will come quickly (v 11; 1:7; 19:11).

6. I will make you a pillar in the temple of my God (v 12).

7. You will never go out but will always have a safe dwelling place (v 12).

8. I will give you God's name (v 12).

9. I will give you the name of the New Jerusalem (v 12).

10. I will give you my new name (v 12).

Revelation 3:14–22

This epistle is to the church of Laodicea. You notice that the church of Laodicea is the only church Jesus had nothing to compliment them on. However, notice the Laodicea had plenty to compliment themselves about:

1. They thought they were rich

2. They were increased in goods

3. They believed they had need for nothing

Jesus counseled them with five things:

1. Buy of me gold tried in the fire (the gold there represents faith 1 Peter 1:7)

2. Buy of me white raiment (white raiment represents righteousness Revelation 19:8)

3. Anoint your eyes with eye-salve (this represents being enlightened by the Holy Spirit and the word of God Psalm 19:8; Ephesians 1:18; Hebrews 6:4; 1 John 2:27)

4. Be zealous to save your souls (Hebrews 12:6–8)

5. Repent

CHAPTER 4

At this point, the rapture has occurred. We know this because the very first verse tells us that John is about to see the *things which must be hereafter.* After the churches!!! The churches are not mentioned again in the Book of Revelations.

The following is proof of the rapture before the tribulation:

1. Luke 21:36, Read

2. John 14:1–3

3. 1 Corinthians 15:51–57

4. Ephesians 5:25–27

5. Philippians 3:11, 20–21; 2 Corinthians 5:1–9

6. 1 Thessalonians 4:13–18; 2:19; 3:13; 5:9, 23

7. 2 Thessalonians 2:1, 7–8

8. Colossians 3:4; 1 John 2:28; 3:2; 1 Peter 5:4

9. James 5:7–8

Remember 1 Thessalonians 5:9, "For God hath not appointed us to wrath, but to obtain salvation by our Lord Jesus Christ." Now couple that with Revelation 6:15–17, Read. Jesus Christ did not cover us so that we would go through the Great Tribulation!!! I am convinced that the church is raptured BEFORE the Great Tribulation.

Revelation 4:4

The word *elder* there is translated from the Greek word *presbuteros*. Remember the Old Testament was originally translated from the Hebrew language to English. The New Testament was originally translated from the Greek language to English.

In the early church, even today, we have elders who are ministers, deacons. You will find examples of these in the

New Testament, (Acts 11:30; 14:23; 16:4; 20:17, 28; 21:18; 1 Timothy 5:17; Titus 1:5; and James 5:14).

The 24 elders represent the raptured church. The proof is that:

1. We know that elder was a position given to the local church.

2. They are distinguished from angels in Revelation 5:11–14.

3. They have crowns and sit on thrones (*the same word translated throne is also translated seat*).

4. They wear white raiment which is only used in Revelation of Christ and saints (Revelation 3:5).

5. We know that one of the elders is a redeemed man showing John the revelation (Revelation 5:5–7; 7:13–15; 19:10; 22:8–9). So, if one of the elders is a redeemed man, then they all are redeemed men who were raptured into heaven.

Revelation 4:6

"A sea of glass" describes the floor of the throne the room of God. The floor is described as being transparent because the word *glass* is used; however, it is not an actual sea as we know a sea to be. The word *sea* is used to describe the vastness of it. Coming from John, this probably meant that it was too large to measure.

Additionally, the word translated *beast* in verse 6 is from the Greek word *Zoa—which means living ones or creatures.* Full of eyes suggests they see everything because we know that sleep is not a requirement in heaven.

Revelation 4:7–9

It is possible the lion represents wild animals, the calf domestic animals, the eagle flying creatures, and man the pinnacle of God's creation.

Isaiah 6:1–7

Seraphim are an order of angelic beings and are only mentioned by name twice in the entire Bible. We see here the similarities between the seraphim and the four beasts:

A. They are both in the throne room.

B. They each have six wings.

C. They each worship the Lord continuously.

The word seraphim means burning ones.

Now knowing what *seraphim* means, we see in Isaiah one of these angelic beings taking a hot coal from the altar and placing it on the mouth of Isaiah.

Additionally, we are told what the six wings (three pairs) are for on these angelic beings.

1. With one pair, they cover their faces (possibly a token of humility).

2. With one pair, they cover their feet (possibly a token of respect).

3. With one pair, they fly (possibly to signify the speed at which they carry out God's commands).

CHAPTER 5

Revelation 5:1–14

Remember the book is in the right hand of *him that sat on the throne* already. Still, John says he saw *a strong angel* inquiring who can open the book. John already knows that angels are supernatural beings, so this angel must have had a physical appearance of strength to get John to describe him as strong.

Keep in mind, John is describing heaven through his eyes at the time. In John's day, a book was really a *scroll.* A scroll was kept rolled up on a stick.

The scroll is a roll of papyrus, leather, or parchment for writing a document.

Papyrus is the pith of the papyrus plant, especially when made into strips and pressed into a material to write on.

Parchment is the skin of a sheep or goat prepared for writing on.

The Lamb took the book from the right hand of God (v 7). The four beasts and 24 elders worship the Lamb with music and incense which in this case represents the prayers of saints.

Verse 6 remember we determined that there is but one Holy Spirit (Ephesians 4:4–6), but we identified seven manifestations of the Holy Spirit in Isaiah 11:2.

Verse 8 Remember we determined by scripture in Chapter 4 that the 24 elders represent the raptured church in heaven. Now, they are each holding a vial (a small glass or plastic container to hold perfume). This represents the prayers of saints. We know that to be a saint, you have to have lived on earth. We also know from scripture that the 24 elders represent the church because they were wearing white raiment, Revelation 4:4, like Jesus, promised the church in Revelation 3:5.

Psalm 141:2, Read

David wrote this Psalm.

We know that the Lamb is Jesus because as mentioned in verse 9, He is our Redeemer. Verse 9 also says *by thy blood out of every kindred, and tongue, and people, and nation.* Now someone tells me who does that leave out? Jesus did not just come for the Jews, even though they thought so, but Jesus came to redeem us all.

Explanation for Revelation 5

In order to fully understand what is occurring here, we must again refer back to the Old Testament because this scroll contains earth's redemption.

Leviticus 25:23–25, Read

35

Lost land could always be redeemed by a kinsman redeemer with the specified redemption price. The provisions were usually written down and sealed in a book that could only be opened by this kinsman redeemer. This kept the transaction a private matter and would not embarrass the family for losing the land.

The seven-sealed scroll contains the terms of redemption for the entire earth. The only one worthy to open it is found in verse 5. We know this is Jesus but notice how he is referred to as being the "Root of David."

Verse 11 Ten thousand was the highest number in ancient Greek. So, when John says *ten thousand times ten thousand, AND thousands of thousands,* he is suggesting a countless or infinite quantity.

CHAPTER 6

Now remember this book had seven seals, Revelation 5:1, but in Chapter 6, we see that only six of the seals were opened (the seventh seal will be opened in Chapter 8). To understand, we must go to:

Daniel 9:24–27

The phrase 70 weeks literally means 70 sevens because there are 7 days in a week. 70 sevens of years because:

1. Daniel's prayer was in reference to years, not days.

2. Daniel 9:25 accounts for 69 weeks ($69 \times 7 = 483$ years).

3. This leaves 1 week of years found in Daniel 9:27, but notice it is divided into two parts. The last 7 is divided *in*

the midst of the week which would make each half 3 ½ years.

See notes above Daniel 9:25, 69 of the 70 weeks have already been accomplished, according to Daniel 9:26, up to the crucifixion of the Messiah.

The 70 weeks or 7 sevens are divided into three main periods:

1. 7 sevens or 49 years for the rebuilding of Jerusalem (v 25)

2. 62 sevens, 434 years from the completion of the city at the end of 49 years to the time the Messiah is crucified.

3. 1 seven, 7 years, of this age, ending with the second Advent of Christ to fulfill the six events (v 24).

The six events of Daniel 9:24 are:

1. To finish the transgression

2. To make an end of sins

3. To make reconciliation for iniquity

4. To bring in everlasting righteousness

5. To seal up the vision and prophecy

6. To anoint the most holy

These six things will be accomplished in the Book of Revelation.

Explanation of Chapter 6

First Seal: Verse 2 is the Antichrist, not Jesus Christ. There are a number of reasons why we know this is not Jesus Christ, but the main reason that resonates with me is the bow. Christ is always symbolized as having a sword, not a bow (Revelation 1:16; 19:15, 21). Keep in mind that the Antichrist is an imitator of Jesus Christ but there are very stark differences in how they arrived on earth.

In comparing:

1. The arrival of Jesus on earth was announced, from heaven, at his birth (Luke 2:8–14). The arrival of the Antichrist

was not announced, thus when the seal was removed the Antichrist went to work immediately.

2. At 12 years old, Jesus knew his purpose (Luke 2:42–49). The seal on the Antichrist prevented the Antichrist from his purpose.

3. At the baptism of Jesus by John the Baptist, God the Father made an announcement from heaven declaring that Jesus was his son (Matthew 3:16–17). The Antichrist was released following the rapture of the church from earth and the Antichrist went forth right away *conquering and to conquer* (Revelation 6:1–2).

The Antichrist was not announced but instead was released by a seal and went to work immediately *conquering and to conquer.*

Second Seal: Verses 34 This horseman is riding a red horse which symbolizes war. This horseman does have a sword, but his horse is not white like the one Jesus Christ will be riding later in Revelation. This war is a direct result of the Antichrist coming on the scene.

Third Seal: Verses 5–6 This horseman is riding a black horse which symbolizes famine. Bread by measure and weight signifies scarcity. Notice *see thou hurt not the olive and the wine* in verse 6. That is because the olive and grape need no cultivation.

Fourth Seal: Verses 7–8 The Greek word *chloros* was translated here to get the word *pale green*. Remember we are in the tribulation, so it is not strange that death and hell come from the same seal. According to verse 8, the war, famine, and death are only affecting a *fourth part* of the earth at this time.

It is currently estimated that the world population is more than 6 billion people. A fourth of this would be approximately one and a half billion. Remember the atomic bomb dropped on Hiroshima, Japan, in 1945? Well, we now have the hydrogen bomb which is 1000 times more potent than the atomic bomb.

In John's day, he could only imagine the possibility of killing off a fourth of the earth's people, but we know the possibilities today. Additionally, because of the famine, there will probably be diseases that follow. Weak and sick people are easy prey for *beasts of the earth* (v 8).

Fifth Seal: Verses 9–11 These are the people who were saved and slain following the rapture and during the first 3 ½ years of the tribulation. Notice they are given white robes (white raiment). Verse 11 makes it clear that others will be saved and killed during the tribulation.

Sixth Seal: Verses 12–17 These events do not mean the extinction of the heavens, sun, moon, stars, mountains, or the islands because these are mentioned later in Revelations.

Notice the seven classes of men who now realize that God's wrath has begun:

1. Kings

2. Great men

3. Rich men

4. Chief captains

5. Mighty men

6. Every bondman

7. Every free man

That did not seem to leave out anyone. Verses 16–17 make it clear that the period of *grace* is over. They are now in the period of *judgments.* Still, some will be saved in the tribulation (v 9–11).

CHAPTER 7

Keep in mind, all of these are following the rapture. The earth is now in judgment. Four angels are positioned in the four directions (N, S, E, and W). A fifth angel instructs the original four angels to wait until 144,000 Jews are sealed, 12,000 from each of the 12 tribes ($12,000 \times 12 = 144,000$). Verse 3 suggests that the 144,000 are still on the earth during the time of tribulation, which means, they were not servants of God at the time of the rapture.

The 12 tribes mentioned in Revelation 7:5–8 are:

1. Juda

2. Reuben

3. Gad

4. Aser

5. Nepthalim

6. Manasses

7. Simeon

8. Levi

9. Issachar

10. Zabulon

11. Joseph

12. Benjamin

The 12 sons or patriarchs of Jacob/Israel found in Genesis 49:1–27 are:

1. Reuben

2. Simeon

3.Levi

4. Judah

5. Issachar

6. Zebulun

7. Gad

8. Asher

9. Dan

10. Naphtali

11. Benjamin

12. Joseph (sons Ephraim and Manasseh)

The tribe of Dan is missing from the list in Revelation. When you go to Genesis 49:1–27, you read about Jacob blessing his 12 sons. Dan is included. Also, when you read Genesis 48, you find Jacob/Israel adopting and blessing Ephraim and Manasseh, the sons of Joseph. Manasseh is mentioned in Revelation and Ephraim is not.

Ezekiel 48:30–35

This is a miniature look at the New Jerusalem that we will study about in Revelation 21. Notice Dan is mentioned here. Remember the Jews have always looked forward to living on earth in a kingdom with the Messiah who we know is Jesus, but the Jews rejected His first coming. It was likely prophecies like this that led the Jews to expect that when Jesus came the first time, He would set up his kingdom on the earth at that time. When this did not happen, the Jews rejected Jesus as being the Messiah. However, their expectation will be met in the millennium or 1000-year reign.

Romans 11:25–32

All Israel shall be saved. Remember that *shall* is a firm word and verse 29 firms it up by explaining that God has not changed His calling on Israel going all the way back to Abraham.

How will God save ALL of Israel in the end???

Ezekiel 37:1–14

The 12 tribes (144,000) who are sealed as servants of God in Revelation 7:5–8 will be with God in Chapter 14.

Verses 9–14 Remember we are in the Great Tribulation. The tribulation is a period of 7 years. The final 3 ½ years are referred to as the *Great Tribulation.* Mentioned here are a multitude of people from all nations and tongues clothed in white robes. Verse 14 is proof that many will be redeemed during the Great Tribulation.

We know from previous teachings that the white robes or raiment represents the redeemed not angels.

CHAPTER 8

Remember the number 7 represents completeness. Now the seventh seal is opened and there is silence in heaven for 30 minutes. Notice how the scripture uses the term *about the space of half an hour.* Keep in mind, there is no time in heaven, but John is describing his experiences in human terms.

Zephaniah 1:7, Read

Zephaniah is prophesizing about *the day of the Lord* which we know now to be the end times; the very time that John was living in and the time we are living in today.

Anno Domini (AD or A.D.) is Latin for *the year of the Lord or in the year of our Lord.*

Verses 2–6 explain the events in heaven before the first trumpet is sounded. This time is referred to as the trumpet judgments.

Exodus 30:7–8, Read

This is why God was so specific to Moses about the instructions first for building the earthly tabernacle and also about his instructions to Aaron the High Priest when it came to conducting business inside the tabernacle. It is because of:

Hebrew 8:5

No interpretation needed.

Verse 7 The first trumpet sounds. Immediately following was *hail and fire mingled with blood,* affecting a third of trees and all green grass.

Verses 8–9 The second trumpet sounds. A burning mountain could be a very large meteor from heaven. Now with the telescope, we can practically see this almost any day of the week, but a large one has not hit earth yet. This affects a third of sea life in the water and ships on the water.

Verses 10–11 The third trumpet sounds. *There fell a great star from heaven; burning as it were a lamp* could be another meteor falling to earth. This meteor made a third part the drinking water bitter. I have heard that now there is a process where raw sewage can be converted into drinking water.

Exodus 15:23–25, Read (bitter water)

Verse 12 The fourth trumpet sounds. Remember Revelation 6:12–13 where it is suggested that the sun, moon, and stars are no more. Now without question, this is affecting a third part of the sun, moon, and stars. Of course, we know this also affected a third part of the day and night.

What we call *daylight saving time* does a similar function for us but because there is no time in heaven, God uses the elements of heaven to affect the change.

Thus far there have been four of seven trumpets to sound. In verse 13, a flying angel is warning with three woes of the three trumpets yet to sound.

CHAPTER 9

Verses 1–2: The fifth trumpet sounds, the first of three woes begins. There is a falling star from heaven, but personal pronouns are used in reference to this fallen star, so we know this is not a meteor. Instead, this is an intelligent being. Additionally, we know this is not a fallen or demonic angel because he is given the key to the bottomless pit to open it.

Verses 3–5: Locusts are released upon the earth, but these are not ordinary locusts because these are told not to eat grass, trees, or any green thing. Remember in Revelation 8:7, all the green grass was burnt up. Notice in verse 4, it is apparent that the grass is still there, but it is not referred to as *green grass.*

Ordinary locust Exodus 10:3–20

Additionally, these locusts are given the command to not hurt the 144,000 who have the seal of God in their foreheads. This same command was given in Revelation 7:3–4. This means that the 144,000 Jews, 12,000 from each of the 12 tribes of Israel, are still on the earth. These locusts torment men on the earth who do not have the seal of God in their foreheads for 5 months.

These demons among other things are described as having faces like men. This means they were intelligent beings, not insects. *The sound of their wings was as the sound of chariots of many horses running to battle.* John probably uses this description because the sound of many chariots was the most fearsome sound in ancient warfare. Remember Israel is under Roman rule at this time and the Romans had one of the best-organized militaries known to man. So, John was very familiar with the sound of many chariots.

Verse 11 tells us these demons have a king and his name in the Hebrew is *Abaddon* and in the Greek *Apollyon.* Both names are translated *destruction.* Referring to this demon as king suggests that he is Satan and according to John 10:10, we know that Satan is the destroyer.

Remember in Revelation 6:2, the Antichrist is released upon the earth. The word released is appropriate because the Antichrist came from the first seal opened by the Lamb.

Verse 13 The sixth trumpet sounds, the second of three woes begins. An unidentified voice speaks from the golden altar. Moses was commanded by God to duplicate this altar in:

Exodus 30:1–18, 37:25–28.

A cubit is about 18 inches and was usually measured by using the forearm from the elbow to the tip of the middle finger.

Verse 14 Four angels are loosed which were bound in the Euphrates River. Two things to point out here are:

1. These are fallen angels because they were bound. Heavenly angels are never bound.

2. The Euphrates River still exists in the region of the Middle East.

Verses 15–16 are talking about a fixed point in time and not just one hour. The third part of man will be slain by these four angels. These four angels control an army of 200 million (200,000,000) horsemen, 50 million each.

Remember at the opening of the fourth seal (Revelation 6:7–8), a fourth of the world's population was killed. Now we read about a third of what is left of the population being killed. Together, this is approximately one-half of the world's population. (Removing a fourth leaves a third and removing one-third from a third leaves one-half). This third of men are killed by the fire, smoke, and brimstone from the mouths of this demonic army.

Verses 20–21 With half of the population already killed, men still do not repent of their evil works to include idol worshiping, murders, sorceries, fornication, and thefts.

The Greek word translated as *sorceries* (Pharmakon, far-mah-kon) is the word from which we get our word "pharmacy," which we know means drugs. This would suggest widespread drug use.

CHAPTER 10

Verses 1–2 Here, we have another mighty angel. We know that all angels are supernatural, and they are all mighty to us but apparently, this distinction is made for a reason.

Verses 5–7 This same mighty angel swears before God *that there should be time no longer.* This is interpreted as the delay in time of fulfillment of the mystery of God will be no longer. In fact, verse 7 is saying just that. In short, the time of waiting is now over.

One thing in particular that God has prolonged over time is the judgment of Satan. The Old Testament prophets did prophecies about his defeat (Isaiah 24:21–22)

Isaiah 25:7–9

When the scripture refers to *his people,* we know it is talking about the nation of Israel. There will be no more rebuke for the nation Israel. Finally, Israel is no longer blinded. We know this because, in verse 9, it Reads, *it shall be said in that day, Lo, this is our God; we have waited for him, and he will save us: this is the LORD; we have waited for him, we will be glad and rejoice in his salvation.*

Verses 8–10 John is told to eat the little book and that it would be sweet in his mouth, but bitter in his belly. In Ezekiel 2:8–3:3, we find a similar experience. These acts actually happened and symbolize the digesting of the word. Digestion makes the word a part of you and your understanding.

This book was first mentioned in Revelation Chapter 5. Remember at that time, they were looking for someone worthy to open the book. This book had seven (7) seals and only the Lamb (Jesus) was able to lose the seals on the book.

The first seal was loosed in Chapter 6 and the seventh seal was loosed in Chapter 8. After the seven seals were loosed from the book by the Lamb, six trumpets were sounded. There are total of seven trumpets, but the seventh trumpet is not sounded until Chapter 11. Now in Chapter 10, we see this mighty angel come down from heaven with the little book now open in his hand.

Verse 11: Now remember John is exiled on the island of Patmos. Yet he is told *"Thou must prophesy again before many peoples, and nations, and tongues, and kings."* The words prophesy means to speak God's message to the people. This will be done in person. The word *again* suggests that John will be required to eventually return to the mainland with the population of people because we know they are not on the island of Patmos.

CHAPTER 11

Verses 1–2 A measuring reed was about 12 ½ feet long and resembled a rod. The city of Jerusalem (the Holy City) will be controlled by the Antichrist for 42 months or 3 ½ years. Remember the entire tribulation is for a period of 7 years.

2 Chronicles 3:1–2 tell us that the original temple was built on Mount Moriah.

The Land of Moriah is the same area where Abraham offered up his son Isaac as a sacrifice, Genesis 22:1–14. The Land of Moriah consists of all the mountains of Jerusalem like Calvary, Zion, Olives, Moriah, and others. According to my study bible, Mount Calvary is the highest peak. Mount Calvary is probably what Abraham saw in Genesis 22:4

when after 3 days into his journey, he *"saw the place afar off."*

Question: What mount was Jesus crucified on???

Answer: Luke 23:33.

David later purchased Mount Moriah in 2 Samuel 24:17–25 and David's son Solomon built the temple there.

Back to Revelation

According to these scriptures, the temple has been rebuilt and is in use during the tribulation. The original temple, built by Solomon, was destroyed by the Romans in about 70 A.D., more than 20 years before John wrote Revelation in 93 A.D. Today as we speak, the temple has not been rebuilt. For it to be rebuilt in its original place, the Dome of the Rock (the third most holy mosque in Islam), which now stands there, would have to be destroyed. Muslims believe the rock in the dome is where Muhammad ascended to heaven in 621 A.D.

Verses 3–4 The names of the two witnesses are not identified here but we know that they are men who will witness for God 1260 days. When you divide 1260 days by 1 year, 365 days, you get approximately 3 ½ years.

Whoever the two witnesses are, they were in heaven when Zechariah prophesied in Zechariah 4:11–14 which was approximately 500 years before Jesus Christ came on the scene. I do not know who the two witnesses are but there have been two men taken to heaven without dying and they are:

1. Enoch in Genesis 5:22–24

2. Elijah in 2 Kings 2:11

These two men were already in heaven when Zechariah came on the scene. This means that it cannot be anyone in the New Testament.

Hebrew 9:27

Now since we know that God's word is true and cannot be changed, keep in mind that all scripture must be fulfilled. Here is your clue:

1. Who are the only two men in the history of man who have not died a natural death without rapture? In order to fulfill the scripture in Hebrew 9:27, these two men must die.

Verses 5–6 For 1260 days (3 ½ years), the two witnesses cannot be harmed. They have the power to kill men with fire spewed from their mouths, to stop the rain, turn water to blood, and to cause plagues to come upon the earth.

Verses 7–12 Following their appointed time of testimony (1260 days or 3 ½ years), they are killed by the beast from the bottomless pit. Their bodies remain in the streets of Jerusalem for 3 ½ days and after 3 ½ days, God reunites their spirit with their bodies. In other words, a resurrection and rapture occur.

The rapture of the two witnesses completes the first resurrection, the resurrection of all the righteous dead BEFORE the millennium. The first resurrection began with the resurrection of Jesus Christ.

1 Corinthians 15:23; 1 Thessalonians 4:13–18

In Corinthians and Thessalonians, it is referring to the resurrection of the righteous.

John 5:28–29

Jesus is talking here, and He is referring to the resurrection of all the righteous and the evil. Eventually, all will be raised and live forever in heaven or Hell.

Verse 13 You still would not hear me say who the two witnesses are but the 7000 killed here is the same number of men reserved to God during Elijah's Old Testament life (1 Kings 19:18; Romans 11:4).

Verse 15 The seventh trumpet is sounded. The woes are the events that follow the sound of the trumpet. Keep in mind, as we go forward from here, the Book of Revelation is revealing both things that will happen and things that have already happened.

Verses 16–17 Remember we determined that the 24 elders represent the New Testament church. Notice how their worship using present tense in *art*, past tense in *wast*, and future tense in *art to come*. I brought that out to validate my previous statement that while Reading Revelation, you must constantly sort between what has already happened and what still has to happen.

Verse 18 The 24 elders are still talking here. Notice the word *Saints* mentioned there. Remember to be a Saint, you must have lived on the earth because Saints were not created in heaven. Also, this scripture is referring to all of the saved,

Old and New Testament. Now remember during the rapture, the wicked were not raised (1 Thessalonians 4:13–18); so, this scripture is still referring to the wicked as dead. The wicked will be judged not by those who love Christ.

Chapter 12

Revelation Chapters 12–14 record an interlude between the sounding of the seventh trumpet (Revelation 11:15) and the beginning of the seven bowls of wrath. These chapters reveal six key personalities who play important roles during the latter part of the Great Tribulation.

This chapter symbolically describes the satanic hatred toward God's plan for Israel. Israel is the bloodline from which the Messiah, Jesus Christ, came from. This chapter is a symbol representing a reality.

Verses 1–2 The woman is symbolic of the nation of Israel. The crown of 12 stars represents the 12 tribes of Israel.

Verses 3–4 describe how Satan and his followers came to be upon the earth. Satan is now a free agent and desires to destroy the man-child. The goal of Satan is to prevent any of God's creation from going to heaven and being with God as God desires.

Verse 5 The man child represents the 144,000 Jews who were sealed with protection from the trumpet judgments. Now the seventh and final trumpet has sounded and the man-child, representing the 144,000, is raptured up to God (Revelation 14:1).

Some may believe that the *Man-Child* here is the birth of Jesus. The following is proof to say that the man-child symbolizes the 144,000 Jews:

1. The sun-clothed woman is not Mary but instead represents the entire nation of Israel. Since the woman represents a nation, a company of people, so must the man-child represent a company of people, the 144,000 Jews.

2. The man-child is not Christ because John is viewing things at the end of Daniel's 70th week, the second half of

the tribulation. We know that Jesus was crucified in the 69th week, followed by the Church Age which has no time limit on it and then the rapture of the church.

Verse 6 The nation of Israel flees Jerusalem the final 3 ½ years of the tribulation often referred to as the Great Tribulation. Remember the first 3 ½ years of the tribulation consisted of the 144,000 Jews who were preaching to the nation of Israel (Revelation 7:3–4). Now during the second 3 ½ years, the Antichrist has taken away his promise of peace with Israel and has occupied the temple. The 144,000 Jews are no longer on the earth because they were raptured in verse 5. The nation of Israel flees from the presence of the Antichrist.

Matthew 24:15–22

Jesus is responding to three questions asked by his disciples in verse 3:

1. When shall these things be?

2. What shall be the sign of thy coming?

3. What shall be the sign of the end of the world?

To understand these scriptures, you must remember that the disciples are Jews, so this answer is specific to them. In these scriptures, Jesus is speaking of the Great Tribulation, the second half of Daniels 70th week. The church is already raptured at this time; so, the elect mentioned in verse 22 is speaking of Israel, because we know Israel is in the tribulation.

Daniel 9:27

The antichrist will turn against Israel in the middle of the 70th week. He will stop the sacrifice and make the temple *desolate* which means people will not be present. Israel flees when the Antichrist turns on them.

Daniel 12:1

The antichrist turning on Israel brings war in heaven and God's people are delivered.

Side Note: An important principle to remember about obtaining victory from God. The victory first occurs in the heavenly rim. Example in Daniel 10:12–13.

Verses 7–9 The Archangel Michael and his angel's war in heaven against the dragon and his angels. Satan is defeated along with one-third of the angels and is cast out to no longer have access to heaven. Read verse 8 again.

Luke 10:18 (Preadamite Period)

Jesus witnessed or was responsible for the casting out of Satan from heaven. This is the original casting out of Satan from heaven for pride. In order to properly explain this, we must explain what scholars refer to as *The Pre-adamite Period* or the time before AD.

We know the Bible speaks of only ONE war in heaven and this war in heaven did not occur until the Great Tribulation and Satan's access to heaven is revoked forever. First, let's prove that Satan had access to heaven before this war in heaven.

Job 1:6–8; 2:1–6

Notice here that Satan had access to heaven after being cast out; the casting out that Jesus was responsible for.

The Pre-adamite Period

Isaiah 14:12–15

Let us pull the nuggets out of this:

Verse 12 Lucifer who is Satan was created a high-ranking angel and these scriptures are describing his position after being cast out. Notice it says that he weakened the nations. Since he was cast out before Adam was created, which is how he came to be on earth when Adam was there, the nations referred to here would have to be nations before Adam.

Verse 13 Here, Lucifer has a throne, but his throne is on earth. Remember he was created as an angel of God and referred to as *the son of the morning*. He was originally created to manage the earth, but instead, he caused the original creation to fall which is why things were so bleak in Genesis Chapter 1. Remember in verse 1, he *weakened the nations*. Also, he attempted to move his throne from earth to heaven. This did not create a war in heaven at this time because he still had access, but he was cast down to earth.

Verse 14 reveals the pride that caused his casting out.

Verse 15 reveals Satan's final judgment.

Jeremiah 4:23–26

This explains the chaos that was on the earth before Adam. The heavens mentioned here are referring to the atmospheric heavens, not the residing heaven where God is. There was no light in the heavens, there was no man, the birds had left, and it had been a fruitful place and had cities.

Ezekiel 28:11–17

This is a prophecy regarding Satan and according to verse 13 having been in the Garden of Eden before Adam. Also, verse 14 refers to this subject as a *cherub* which we know to be angels. Verse 17 refers to his brightness and in Isaiah 14:12

he is referred to as the *son of the morning*. Again, we see that Satan's assignment was to be in charge of the earth.

2 Peter 3:5–8

These scriptures are clear and alone was enough to convince me of a *Preadamite period.*

Verse 5 proves that God spoke the old heavens, not the residential heaven where God lives, and the earth into existence by His word. This is before the activity in Genesis. Notice *the earth standing out of the water and in the water.* This means that the earth was not completely flooded in its original creation before Genesis.

Verse 6 World here is translated from the Greek word *kosmos* which means *social system.* So, this verse could be translated *the social system that then was, being overflowed with water, perished.*

We know this is not talking about the flood during Noah's time because the social system was preserved by Noah's family. Not so before Genesis Chapter 1.

Verse 7 The current heavens and earth, the one we live in now, will be judged by fire, remembering twice before the earth was destroyed by water.

Psalms 104:5–9

Verse 5 God created the earth as a permanent fixture.

Verse 6 is speaking of the flood before Genesis, not the flood of Noah. We know this because of verse 7. God rebuked the waters in Genesis with His voice or word. This did not occur during the flood of Noah. Instead, during Noah's time, the waters naturally receded over a period of 150 days (Genesis 8:1–3).

Verses 8–9 At the time of Genesis Chapter 1, God did not intend to allow another flood, but during Noah's time, sin got out of hand again and God did flood the earth once more. The exception during Noah's time is that God promised Noah with a rainbow that He would not destroy the earth by water a third time (Genesis 9:11–17).

Genesis 1:27–28

Here, God told Adam and Eve to *be fruitful, and multiply, replenish the earth.* The word *replenish* is key here because it suggests that the earth was once populated BEFORE Adam.

Back to Revelation 12 (end of the preadamite period of study)

Verses 10 Notice in these verses the Devil is referred to as the *accuser.* Verses 11–14 The devil will severely persecute Israel the final 3 ½ years of the tribulation.

Verses 15–16 The armies of the antichrist will pursue after Israel, but the earth will help by swallowing up the armies.

Numbers 16:29–34

God has opened the ground before the tribulation. God can certainly do it during the tribulation.

Verse 17 Satan wars against those of Israel who do not flee into the wilderness. Remember verse 6 those in the wilderness are cared for. Those left behind appear to have converted to Christianity. This could be because they witnessed the 144,000 Jews raptured to heaven in Revelation 12:5; 14:1.

CHAPTER **13**

Remember Chapters 12–14 record an interlude, a period of time between events.

Verse 1 The sea here is likely symbolic of people because the beast is a man who will rise up out of the sea of humanity. This beast represents the rise of the Antichrist to power, and according to verse 18 in this chapter, he is a man. The seven heads represent seven kingdoms (Revelation 17:9–10). The 10 horns and 10 crowns represent 10 kingdoms to come under the Antichrist's control later (Revelation 17:12–13).

Daniel 7:19–21

This speaks of the 10 kingdoms represented by 10 horns. There is another horn that comes up, the Antichrist, and conquers 3 of the 10 kingdoms.

As we go forward, we must keep in mind that the extent of the Antichrist's control during this time is 10 kingdoms within the Old Roman Empire.

This horn, the Antichrist, made war with the saints and overcame them, Revelation 13:7. These saints are those who are converted to Christianity on the earth during the Great Tribulation. We know this because the Antichrist is not in heaven making war.

Verse 2 The leopard symbolizes the Grecian Empire; the bear symbolizes the Medo-Persia Empire, and the lion symbolizes the Babylonian Empire. The dragon was identified in Revelation 12:9 as Satan, the Devil, and an old serpent.

Verse 3 We are told in Revelation 17:9–10 that the seven heads represent seven kingdoms. Now with that in mind, one of the heads is wounded to death and this head of the beast is healed. The beast here is representative of the Antichrist. Following this head being healed *All* the world wondered after the beast.

You could believe this is referring to a literal head like mine or yours that was wounded and healed, or you can go with what we already know. These heads represent kingdoms, and this could be referring to the Antichrist reviving one of the seven kingdoms that was in bad economic condition. Reviving a country from economic ruin would certainly gain the attention of the world, just a thought.

Additionally, remember the tribulation will be worldwide. Though the Antichrist will theoretically be based somewhere in the area of the Old Roman Empire, his influence will likely be far-reaching.

Verse 4 The Antichrist got his power from Satan.

Verses 5–6 The Antichrist speaks against God for 3 ½ years (42 months).

Verse 7 The Antichrist is *him* in this scripture. The Antichrist is given power purposed to overcome the Saints in the Great Tribulation but knows that he is not successful in doing so. Remembering that the Antichrist's rule is limited to the 10 kingdoms within the Old Roman Empire, the *All* here only refers to that portion of the world.

Verse 8–9 The word *foundation* is translated from the Greek word *katabole* which means to overthrow or cast down. Notice world is used there also, which is translated from the Greek word *kosmos* which means the social world.

This refers to the overthrow of the preadamite world by the first flood of Genesis 1:2.

The similar wording in Matthew 13:35 may help us to understand this translation better.

Verse 10 This could be interpreted as He that is destined to captivity will go into captivity; he that is destined to the sword will be killed by the sword.

Verses 11–12 This second beast is the false prophet. Because of the pronoun "He," we know this is a man and he does the bidding of the Antichrist. Remember the Antichrist was the first beast.

So now in this chapter, we have the unholy trinity represented:

1. The dragon—Satan

2. The Antichrist

3. The false prophet

2 Thessalonians 2:3–4

These verses are referring to the revealing of the Antichrist and verse 3 further proves that he will be a man and not an actual beast.

Verses 13–15 The prophet, or second beast, caused an image to be made of the first beast, the Antichrist. The prophet performed numerous miracles to include, making fire come down from heaven and giving life to the image of the Antichrist. Those who would not worship the image could be killed.

There are numerous scriptures in the bible where God rained fire from heaven: Genesis 19:24; 2 Kings 1:10–14; 1 Chronicles 21:26; 2 Chronicles 7:1; Job 1:16.

1 Kings 18:30–38

God proves himself by fire from heaven to the nation Israel. Remember many Jews will be in the tribulation and they have these scriptures and they believe these scriptures. The Great Tribulation will be so terrible that some may relate to what is happening with the Old Testament scripture.

Verses 16–18 Notice that verse 17 refers to the mark as:

1. The mark or

2. The name of the beast (Antichrist) or

3. The number of his name

This signifies that whatever the mark will be, it will be a representation of the Antichrist. We know now that the first beast is the Antichrist.

Verse 18 gives us the number of the mark as 666. This does not necessarily mean that the mark will be 666 because, in the Greek and Hebrew alphabets, there is not a separate system of numbers, as in the English language. The letters of the Greek and Hebrew languages represent numbers.

The letters in the name of the future Antichrist will have a numerical value of 666 and this mark would not be implemented until the second half of Daniel's 70th week (the last 3 ½ years of the tribulation or the Great Tribulation).

Review questions/what or who is:

1. The Great Tribulation (last 3 ½ years) began in Chapter 12.

2. The sun-clothed woman represents the nation Israel.

3. The dragon represents Satan.

4. The male child represents the chosen 144,000 Jews.

5. Michael the Archangel is the leader of God's angels.

6. The first beast represents the Antichrist.

7. The second beast represents the false prophet.

8. The dragon represents Satan.

CHAPTER **14**

Verse 1 This is Mount Zion in heaven because the Lamb is standing with the 144,000 who were raptured into heaven in Revelation 12:5.

Verses 2–3 John heard the 144,000 singing a song that only they could sing. Imagine a choir of 144,000 singing so beautifully that it sounds like one voice. That is what John heard and they were playing harps. Also, remember these are Jews.

Additionally, verse 3 says that these 144,000 were *redeemed* from the earth, further proof that they were raptured following the first 3 ½ years of the tribulation and before the later 3 ½ years.

Verses 4–5 This makes it clear that the 144,000 are men when the scripture says *they were not defiled by women.* Yes, men can be virgins. We know the 144,000 referenced here are Jews redeemed or raptured from the earth during the tribulation.

Notice they are referred to as the *first fruits unto God and to the Lamb/Jesus Christ.* The word *firstfruits* brings notice to the fact that these are the first Jews raptured during the tribulation and following the rapture of the church in Revelation 4.

Verses 6–7 An angel is going to and fro in heaven preaching the gospel to those who still dwell on the earth with a new twist. This angel is preaching that *the hour of God's judgment is come.* For centuries, we have only been able to say that *the hour of God's judgment is coming.* We see God's mercy at work again trying to prevent men from taking the mark of the Antichrist, because he who takes the mark cannot be saved (verses 9–11).

Verse 8 Remember Revelation Chapters 12–14 is an interlude. This announcement is being made in heaven even though the fall of Babylon on earth does not actually occur until Chapter 17. This is a good example of God's will being accomplished in heaven first, then earth.

Matthew 6:10

This is the Lord's Prayer and an outline of how Jesus told us to pray. Because of this and other examples, I believe that when we pray, our victory is first announced in heaven and then manifested to us on the earth. We know God is not hard of hearing as Daniel discovered in Daniel 10:12–13.

Verses 9–11 A third angel is flying in heaven preaching loudly warning the people on earth not to receive the mark of the beast in their foreheads. The people on earth are warned of everlasting torment of fire and brimstone if they worship the Antichrist and take his mark.

Verses 12–13 These verses are speaking of those who hold to their faith during the Great Tribulation. Notice they are referred to as saints. Remember to be a saint, you have to have lived on earth because saints are not created in heaven. These scriptures make it plain that some will be saved during the Great Tribulation and many will be killed for not worshiping or taking the mark of the Antichrist.

Because many will be killed for not receiving the mark of the beast, this scripture says *blessed are the dead which die in the Lord from henceforth.*

2 Corinthians 5:8

A person who dies in the Lord (absent from the body) will, in spirit, be immediately present with the Lord. This is just another example of there being NO conflict in the word of God. This scripture is in total agreement with what we just Read in Revelation 14:13.

Verses 14–16 The Son of man, wearing a crown in this verse, is Jesus holding a sharp sickle in his hand. Now notice in verses 15 and 17, angels are coming forth from a temple which is in heaven. There is a temple in heaven, but so as not to confuse anyone, let us Read:

Revelation 21:22–23

This clearly says that there will not be a temple, but this is talking about the New Jerusalem which will be set up on earth and there will not be a sun or moon because the glory of God and the Lamb will lighten it.

Additionally, to explain that *the Son of man* here is Jesus, we will refer to some scriptures:

Matthew 12:8; 13:41; 16:27; John 1:51

Jesus is talking in all four of these scriptures and the list goes on. If you have an electronic bible, you can search these scriptures with the keywords "Son of Man."

Still, in verse 15, we have determined that the one sitting on the white cloud is Jesus. So, who is giving the angel instructions from the temple? Jesus is sitting on the cloud and is not in the temple at this time. It is almighty God the Father!!!

Revelation 16:17 proves that the throne of God the Father is in the temple of heaven. Again, it is almighty God the Father directing the events in heaven during the tribulation.

Matthew 24:36; Acts 1:7

What these scriptures are telling us is that God the Father controls the timing of everything, especially the decisions being made in heaven regarding the end during the tribulation.

Verses 17–20 Remember Chapters 12–14 have been an interlude or a period of time between events. These verses are making reference to the battle of Armageddon even though the battle does not occur until Revelation 19.

This is just another example of preparation for victory being made in heaven before the victory is revealed on earth.

Verse 20 1600 furlongs is about 184 miles. This suggests the enormous armies that will face the Lord at Armageddon.

CHAPTER 15

Verse 1 is a continuation of God's wrath on earth that began in Revelation 6:12. We also learn that this is the last of the plagues which means an end is coming. We have learned from this study that the number 7 is a significant number in heaven. It is mentioned twice in this verse of the 54 times total that it is mentioned in the Book of Revelation.

Additionally, the word *filled* used here is translated from the Greek word *teleo* which means *to complete or bring to an end.*

The word *wrath* used here is translated from the Greek word *thumos* which means *hot anger.*

With both these definitions, we should get the understanding that this is the start of the completeness of God's anger. After all, this is the final half of the tribulation and there are people on earth who are actually worshipping the Antichrist evidenced by taking his mark.

Verse 2 We learned in Revelation 4:6 that this sea of glass is before the throne of God. John again here is trying to describe what he is seeing in human terms, which is why he says, *I saw as it were.* Interpreted *it looked as though* it were *a sea of glass mingled with fire.*

We cannot begin to imagine what the glory of God will look like. Has anyone ever heard of the "Northern Lights?" I have only seen them on television, but at certain times of the year in certain parts of the world, flashes of color can be seen in the sky. To some, this can look like flashes of flames. In any case, it is beautiful. The difference in the Northern Lights and a rainbow is the rainbow is stationary, but the Northern Lights are moving with flashes of color.

Still, in verse 2, everyone who *did not* worship the Antichrist, his image, or take his mark is before the throne and each has a harp.

I see a pattern here. Remember in Revelation 14:1–5, the 144,000 Jews were redeemed from the earth and each possessed a harp in heaven. Now in Revelation 15:2, these are *them that had gotten the victory over the Antichrist, and over his image, and over his mark, and over the number of his name* standing before the throne of God with harps. These are not just Jews in this group but anyone who has overcome.

Remember in Revelation 14:9–11, any man who *worshiped the beast (Antichrist) and his image and receive his mark in his forehead or in his hand* would be tormented with fire and brimstone for eternity. Interpreted this person would not be saved.

There is only one place that I can think of where this judgment can be executed, in Hell the place created for Satan and his angels.

Verse 3 The song of Moses is regarding the defeat of Pharaoh's army in the Red Sea, a song of triumph (Exodus 15:1–19). The song of the Lamb is also a song of triumph, victory over Satan and all enemies of God and man. A few of the words to this song are mentioned here with how *great and marvelous thy works are, Lord God Almighty; just and true are thy ways, thou King of saints.*

Verse 4 The redeemed are in the throne room of God singing praises, playing harps, and worshiping God. We know that God the Father and our Lord Jesus Christ are both in the throne room (Revelation 5:6–7) unless the scripture specifies otherwise as we saw in Revelation 14:14 when Jesus was sitting upon a white cloud outside the temple.

Ephesians 1:15–23 followed by an explanation:

Paul the Apostle wrote the book of Ephesians. Paul starts out by telling them that he has heard of their faith in Jesus and their love for the saints. I find it interesting how Paul explains two persons of the Trinity and how he manages to keep their identities separate.

Verse 17 Paul mentions *the God of our Lord Jesus Christ.* So, we know Paul is referring to God the Father as the subject here.

Verses 18–20 In these verses, God the Father is still the subject of the pronouns *His* and *He* because in verse 20, the *He* there raised Christ from the dead and set him (Christ) at His (God the Father) own right hand in the heavenly places. Notice God the Father did not promote Jesus above himself but to sit next to God the Father.

Verse 21 However, the name of Jesus is promoted above every name now and forever.

The reason for this is explained in:

Verses 22–23 Jesus is Lord over the church (us) because we are His body. Jesus sacrificed His body for us the church. Therefore, God the Father has given Jesus charge over us.

Back to Revelation Chapter 15

Verse 5 The temple in heaven is opened again. The last time was in Revelation 11:19.

Verse 6 By this verse, we know that when John saw these seven angels with the seven plagues in verse 1, they were still in the temple because here they are just now coming out. Notice the dress of these angels *clothed in pure and white linen.* This dress represents the promise given to the church in Revelation 3:5. In Revelation 21:9, one of these seven angels with the *seven vials full of the seven last plagues* mentioned in verse 6 began to show John things in heaven. This tour continues into Revelation 22:8–9; at this point, John fell at the feet of this angel to worship and this angel explains to John that he is a brother and should not be worshiped.

Interpreted this is a man but he came out of the temple of God and is called an angel and is dressed in white linen like the redeemed church. There is a song that we sing in worship and praise services which has lyrics about us *singing with the angels*. The next time you sing that song, I urge you to think about these scriptures.

Verse 7 We have shown with scripture that these seven angels are redeemed, men. Now they each are given vials *full of the wrath of God.* Now, remember these angels received only the final seven plagues from within the temple and now have exited the temple.

Outside the temple, one of the four beasts who we know have been around the throne (Revelation 4:6) gave each of the seven angels a vial *full of the wrath of God.* What I find significant here is that the vials containing the anger of God, which we know is fierce by this time, are not presented to these angels inside the temple of God.

1 Corinthians 6:2

Please hear what the Apostle Paul is saying because the seven angels in Revelation 15 who we now know are redeemed men have been authorized to pour out the wrath of God on the earth during the tribulation. Remember they were given seven last plagues inside the temple and given the vials full of God's wrath on the outside of the temple. These redeemed men are in effect serving up the judgments of God. Keep in mind that terms like redeemed, saints, the church, and Christians are all referring to us. One day, we will be able to add "angel" to this list!!!

Verse 8 suggests that redeemed men are usually able to enter the temple but, in this case, not until after the judgment of the seven plagues is fulfilled. We know this is the temple in

heaven because God the Father is there.

CHAPTER 16

Verse 1 A *great voice* is heard from the temple. This signifies a voice of authority, not just a loud voice. Remember we learned that the throne is in the temple in heaven (Revelation 16:17). Each of these seven angels has a vial full of God's wrath to pour out on the earth.

Wrath—extreme anger; strong vengeful anger; retributory punishment for an offense or a crime: divine chastisement.

The wrath of God began in Revelation 6:12–17 with the opening of the sixth seal. We learned in Chapter 15 that this is the last of the plagues and wrath of God. At this time, some people have taken the mark of the Antichrist and are worshipping the Antichrist and his image.

Verse 2 The first vial poured up the earth causes sores to come upon those who possess the mark of the beast and those who worship his image. Remember this beast referred here is the Antichrist.

Keep in mind, this is happening during the Great Tribulation (the last 3 ½ years) of the 7-year tribulation. Notice this wrath is designed to cause sores upon the men who worship the Antichrist, his image, and who take the mark. Additionally, we learned in Revelation 14:9–11 that anyone who took the mark or worshiped the Antichrist, or his image would not be saved. So, these men are already condemned according to the scriptures we have Read.

The word *noisome* in verse 2 means to be offensive to the senses, especially to the sense of smell; highly obnoxious or objectionable; and very unpleasant or disgusting.

With this in mind, these sores could cause infection and rotten flesh which would, in turn, be offensive to the sense of smell.

Additionally, verse 2 lends to the possibility that these final judgments of God's wrath are concentrated in the territory directly controlled by the Antichrist. Notice the first vial of wrath poured out on the earth affects, primarily those who have the mark of the Antichrist and those who worship the image of the Antichrist.

Verse 3 The second vial of wrath is poured out on the sea. Something similar happened in Revelation 8:8–9, but only one-third of the creatures died then, now with this pouring out of wrath everything dies in the sea.

Verse 4 The third vial of wrath is poured upon the rivers and bodies of fresh water turning them into blood, in other words, the drinking water.

Verse 5 The third angel speaks regarding this judgment of turning the fresh water to blood. This angel exalts God for His righteous judgment on those who *have shed the blood of saints and prophets*.

Verse 6 Keep in mind, this is happening during the second half of the tribulation. The Antichrist has been responsible for the deaths of many saints and in Revelation 13:7, the Antichrist was given the power to make war with the saints.

Verse 7 Another angel is heard speaking from the altar confirming what the third angel with the vial has said that God's judgments are true and righteous. The altar is in the temple and so is the throne of God.

The principal of confirming an act before two or three witnesses is in play here. The following are scriptures confirming this principle in the word of God: Deuteronomy 17:6; 2 Corinthians 13:1; 1 Timothy 5:19; Hebrews 10:28; Revelation 11:3. This should tell us that even God Almighty does not operate outside of His word.

Verses 8–9 The fourth vial is poured out on the sun bringing about scorching heat on those persons still on the earth. Remember these are the hardcore sinners. Notice they do not repent and instead blasphemed the name of God, the exact reaction of the Antichrist when He came on the scene.

Also, notice that repentance is a requirement here. This is important because I have heard modern-day teachers telling people that repentance is not a requirement. This kind of teaching is supported by these teachers also teaching "once saved always saved."

To me, the solution is simple for anyone left behind following the rapture: If you thought you were saved under the once saved always saved teaching and you are left behind scrap it, repent and get it right. Remember in previous chapters, we have already studied that there will be plenty of truth teaching during the first half of the tribulation.

Question: What three factions will be preaching these truths?

Answer: The 144,000 Jews, the two witnesses, and the angel in Revelation 14:6–7.

Verses 10 The fifth vial is poured out upon the seat of the beast or the Antichrist. We know this beast is the Antichrist because *his kingdom was full of darkness*. The second beast of Revelation 13 is the false prophet and the false prophet had no kingdom. Those with sores are now in darkness and suffering from extreme pain to the extent that they *gnawed their tongues for pain.*

Remember the story in the bible where the disciples got in a boat and the storm came up while they were on the lake. I have been on the ocean on a ship when it was cloudy. The darkness was so thick I could not see my hand before my face. Keep in mind, large bodies of water get their color from the sky, so the water is a reflection of the fierceness of the storm.

Verse 11 The sores and pain still do not bring about repentance. Instead, they continue to blaspheme God as they did in verse 9. Notice the need to repent is mentioned twice in this chapter. Repentance is apparently important. Here, we are told that they need to repent of their deeds.

Verse 12 The sixth vial is poured out upon the Euphrates River. The Euphrates River was in the Garden of Eden during Adam's time (Genesis 2:14). The Euphrates River still exists today and will be the eastern border of the Antichrist's kingdom. We are told here that the Euphrates River will be dried up making a way for the kings of the east. It is clear that these kings will be in control of kingdoms apart from the Antichrist's kingdom, further confirming that the Antichrist's kingdom will be contained to a particular territory, the Old Roman Empire. There is a war coming that we will talk about in later chapters.

Verse 13 This is happening following the sixth vial of God's wrath being poured out and before the seventh vial is poured. John says he saw three unclean spirits that looked like frogs: one from the dragon, one from the Antichrist, and one from the false prophet. Here, the unholy three are mentioned in one verse. Notice also they are mentioned in the order of their authority to each other.

The unholy trinity are all mentioned and identified in this same order in Revelation 13. The dragon is the devil who we know gave power to the beast (Revelation 13:4). The first beast mentioned in Revelation 13:2 is the Antichrist. The second beast mentioned in Revelation 13:11 is the false prophet.

Verse 14 These spirits are devils purposed to convince the other kings of the earth to join the army of the Antichrist in battle. These spirits will possibly persuade these kings through unwise counsel. This is not the first time this has been done in the bible.

2 Chronicles 18:18–22 and 1 Kings 22:15–23

This is an example of God allowing a lying spirit to persuade Ahab King of Israel and Jehoshaphat King of Judea, through the Advice of their prophets or Advisors, to enter into a battle that they were destined to lose. We know that this lying spirit was most likely a demonic spirit permitted by God to do this because God cannot lie. I encourage you to Read this story.

Additionally, verse 14 is further proof that the Antichrist will not rule the whole world. It is true as we see here the influence of the Antichrist will be widespread because it clearly says that the devil spirits will influence the kings of the earth and the whole world to bring them to the final battle.

Verse 15 This verse is red lettered in my bible. Jesus is talking here and the "He" in this verse are those who become believers during the tribulation.

Jesus is referring to His second advent. You will not find the word *advent* in the bible, but this is referring to the time when Jesus Christ returns to rule on the earth for a thousand years.

You would not find the word *rapture* in your bible either, but this refers to Jesus' return to take the church out to be with Him in heaven. However, the difference in the rapture and the Second advent is that in the rapture, Jesus will not touch the earth.

In the rapture of the church, Jesus will NOT touch the earth, while in the Second advent, Jesus sets up His kingdom on the earth and rules for a thousand years. So, chronologically speaking first:

1. Jesus (Messiah) has been to earth and provided salvation (even though many Jews think of Him as just a prophet and not the savior).

2. Jesus will return to the sky for the rapture of the church, but will not touch the earth.

3. Jesus will return to earth during the Second advent and set up His kingdom in the New Jerusalem.

Verse 16 The word "He" in this verse is a very important pronoun. In verse 14 the three devil spirits which go forth unto the kings of the earth and of the whole world, to gather them to the battle of that great day of God Almighty.

So, the "He" in that verse is likely talking about the devil. God has chosen the place of battle in verse 12 of this chapter by drying up the water of the Euphrates River to prepare the way for the kings of the east, but in verse 14, the devil is gathering the kings on earth and the whole world to the battle of Armageddon. God prepared the way, but the devil is gathering the kings of the earth for the battle of Armageddon.

Keep in mind, this is the latter half of the tribulation. Jesus will not use anyone still on the earth at this time to fight at Armageddon. However, the devil army will come from those still on the earth.

The devil does not have resurrection power, so his army will be live people, flesh, influenced by the devil spirits!!!

Verse 17 This verse answers a couple of questions: TEST!

1. Revelation 16:17 Where is the temple of God located?

2. Revelation 16:17 Where is the throne of God located?

3. Revelation 14:15 Who is giving instructions from the temple?

4. Revelation 14:15 Who is not in the temple, but sitting on a white cloud?

Answers:

1. Heaven

2. In the temple

3. God the Father

4. Jesus

Remember there were seven angels with a vial each of the wrath of God. Now the seventh angel has poured out his vial in the air. Notice *a great voice came out of the temple of heaven, from the throne, saying, it is done.* Because we have proven that it was God the Father giving the instructions from the temple and this voice came from the throne in the temple, I believe this is the voice of God the Father.

The phrase "a great voice" is mentioned for a distinction of this voice from other voices. I found several scriptures in Revelation using the phrase "a great voice;"

Revelation 1:10–11 (Jesus)

Revelation 11:12 This "great voice" is heard by the two witnesses following the spirit of God entering into them and their resurrection.

Revelation 16:1 (God the Father, because the throne is in the temple)

Revelation 16:17 (God the Father)

Revelation 19:1 (saved people in heaven)

Revelation 21:2–3 This is one voice, probably God the Father because God the Father prepared the New Jerusalem.

Verse 2 tells us the New Jerusalem is *coming down from God out of heaven.*

Verse 18 This indeed is a great earthquake, the result of the seventh vial of God's wrath being poured out. This is the same earthquake mentioned in Revelation 11:13. We know this because this earthquake occurs *the same hour* following the resurrection of the two witnesses and their ascension into heaven.

The mentioning of the earthquake in Revelation 11:13 is known as a *parenthetical (par-en-thet-i-cal) passage.* This is because there are very few details of its destruction until Revelation 16:18–20.

Verse 19 This earthquake will divide the *great city* into three parts and destroy many other cities to include *great Babylon.* The great city that will be divided into three parts is Jerusalem. Babylon would come under *the cities of the nations.*

Revelation 11:8

Here, reference is made to the *great city* previously. We know with certainty that this is Jerusalem because it is where our Lord was crucified.

Verses 20 Keep in mind, the greatest earthquake known to man is occurring at this time. So, it is feasible that the islands and mountains are disappearing.

Verse 21 Hail is falling from heaven each one the weight of a talent which is approximately 114 pounds. Here, they are in the final years of the tribulation and instead of repenting men will blaspheme God.

CHAPTER **17**

Verse 1 This is referring to the same seven angels who came out of the temple in Revelation 15:1. This angel calls John up for a tour. The great whore in this verse is not a woman but a religious system. The waters in this verse represent people. As I explained this before, these seven angels are redeemed men.

Revelation 22:8–9 You should already have in your notes from chapter 15.

Revelation 19:10, Read

Remember when John saw the seven men come out of the Temple in heaven with the seven plaques, they appeared to be angels to him. In Revelation 17:1, one of the seven angels called John up to heaven to show him the judgment of the *great whore that sitteth upon many waters.*

Here, we Read that John fell at his feet to worship him as John did in Revelation 22:8–9; however, the angel told John again not to worship him for *I am thy fellow servant, and of thy brethren that have the testimony of Jesus: worship God: for the testimony of Jesus is the spirit of prophecy.*

Revelation 12:17

John is told something similar regarding those of the nation of Israel who are left behind in the tribulation. It is apparent that at some point, some did begin to keep the *commandments of God* and afterward received *the testimony of Jesus Christ.*

The two questions that beg to be answered is what or who is the spirit of prophecy? And, how does a person obtain the testimony of Jesus Christ? The answer is found in:

John 15:26

First let us not overlook the very important fact that the former disciple, now the Apostle John, the same writer of the Book of Revelation, wrote this scripture. Additionally, this scripture is red lettered in my bible, which means that Jesus is speaking.

Here, Jesus explains it clear that the Holy Spirit will testify of him. The Holy Spirit is "the Spirit of Prophecy" mentioned in Revelation 19:10. It is very important that we also understand that the comforter/spirit of truth is the same spirit who resides in those of us who are saved by the blood of Jesus Christ. Without the Holy Spirit, there is NO testimony of Jesus Christ.

So, what the angel was trying to tell John in Revelation 19:10 is that he is *of thy brethren that have the testimony of Jesus*. We, the redeemed, are of those brethren. We cannot blame John for desiring to worship this redeemed man who John initially identified as an angel in the scripture, but the angel made it clear here who he is.

We talk about the transformation when we come together with Jesus Christ upon His return during the first resurrection. Scriptures like this one (Revelation 19:10) just helps me to understand that our transformation will be so complete that a man, in this case, John, will not be able to see the difference in a redeemed man and an angel.

Examples of a religious system being compared to harlots and whoredom can be found in Jeremiah 3:2–9 and Ezekiel 20:30–32, Read. In these scriptures, the nations of Israel and Judah are spoken of as though they are women and compared to harlots committing whoredom.

Verse 2 This religious system, during the great tribulation, has influenced the kings of the earth or leaders on the earth at this time. Keep in mind with the Church taken from the earth and the mark of the Antichrist now being a requirement to live, any evil is possible.

Just a reminder of what initially set America apart from any other country was the separation of church and state. In other words, our constitution prohibits the government from creating a religion or prohibiting free expression of religious beliefs.

During the tribulation, there will not be any such restrictions. Evidenced by the requirement to worship the statue of the Antichrist and receive his mark on the body.

Verse 3 Remember in verse 1 John is being shown *the judgment of the great whore*. We have determined that this represents the religious system during the tribulation.

The woman in this verse represents this same religious system. The beast the woman is sitting upon is the Antichrist.

We know this because of the 7 heads and 10 horns. We Read about this in Revelation 13:1. It appears that the Antichrist government and the religious system have merged together. Verse 4 Suggests that the followers of this religion will be following after things and wealth. Remember by this time, the Antichrist has moved into the temple of God and taken over. Any true believers have fled the temple to avoid the mark and prosecution and possible death.

Believers are told several times in scripture that we should not pursue *filthy lucre*; 1 Timothy 3:3, 3:8; Titus 1:7, 1:11; 1 Peter 5:2.

Lucre is interrupted as meaning doing something for money or profit. We see some of that now in the church which is why God placed it in the scriptures.

Verse 5 Notice there are three different names *upon her forehead:*

1. Mystery, Babylon the Great

2. The Mother of Harlots

3. Abominations of the Earth

The word Mystery identifies this woman with the religious rites and mysteries of ancient Babylon. The ancient Babylonian cult was started by King Nimrod and Queen Semiramis. The objects of worship in this ancient religion were the supreme Father, the incarnate Female, or Queen of Heaven, and her Son. They made their confessions to priests. In about 63 B.C., Julius Caesar became the head of the Roman branch of the Babylonian Cult.

The name Mother of Harlots identifies the whore as a religious system. The word Harlots refer to the many branches which have sprung up from this religious system. Notice also this is happening after the rapture of the Church. We find God in the Old Testament comparing the pagan religions, followed by Israel, using terms like *adulterer, whoredom, harlot, and whore.*

Isaiah 57:3–7; Jeremiah 3:6–9; Ezekiel 20:30–32; Ezekiel 23:1–12; Hosea 4:12–19; Nahum 3:4.

Ezekiel 20:30–32, Read

It is clear here that the scripture is talking about the nation of Israel and that they are guilty of worshipping idols of wood and stone. We are told that they commit whoredom when they do this.

The name Mother of Abominations of the Earth suggests that this religious system will exceed all others before it in wickedness. Keep in mind there will be worship of the Antichrist and the statue (idolatry). There will be murder and martyrs made of those who refuse to worship the Antichrist or take the mark. And this will be done in mass numbers. The word abomination is used throughout the Bible to identify idol worship.

Deuteronomy 18:9–12; 29:16–18; 32:15–18, Read

Keep in mind that Israel is the only righteous nation in the Old Testament. Now compare that to the rapture having already occurred in the Book of Revelation, meaning there is no church on the earth. We know from Reading the Old Testament that even the nations who did not know the true and living God created Gods from wood and stone.

In these verses in Deuteronomy, the nation of Israel is first warned not to worship the Gods of other nations. These verses in Deuteronomy progress from warning the nation of Israel to punishing them for abominations of worship.

Verse 6 The saints, those who accepted the Lord Jesus Christ as their personal Savior, are killed for not participating in the rituals of this religious system.

Verse 7 The beast referred to here with 7 heads and 10 horns is the Antichrist. This confirms what we recently Read in Revelation 17:3. You may also reread Revelation 13 to be refreshed about the unholy trinity. In Chapter 13, the Antichrist is the first beast, the second beast is the prophet, and the dragon or devil is mentioned in Revelation 13:4.

Verse 8 The first time the bottomless pit is mentioned is in Revelation 9:1 when a heavenly angel is given the key to the bottomless pit and opens it. Demons are released, and they have a king over them we are told in Revelation 9:11 who is called "Abaddon" in the Hebrew and "Apollyon" in the Greek. As we learned when reviewing Revelation Chapter 9 previously, both names are translated to mean destruction. What is important to point out here is that the bottomless pit is not hell because there is no mention of the lake of fire here. We do know that it is a place of restraint because it was secured by a key.

The word perdition in this verse is defined as the state of being in hell forever as punishment after death; eternal damnation.

However, this is a prediction that the beast, which was released from the bottomless pit, will have a final destination of hell. Remember the Great White Throne of judgment has not occurred at this time, so no one is condemned to hell, the lake of fire, and brimstone, at this time.

In order to understand the meaning of the phrase "whose names were not written in the book of life from the foundation of the world," we have to go back to:

Revelation 13:8, Read

This is reminding us that the plan of salvation, to include the sacrifice/crucifixion of Jesus, was prepared and planned before the *foundation of the world.* This also means even before the pre-adamite world.

Hebrew 4:3

This verse is telling us that God already knows the outcome of those who will be saved and those who will not because *the works were finished from the foundation of the world.*

The word world here, many times, is referring to the social system. Remember the earth was only created once, which is why Genesis 1:1 Reads, "In the beginning God created the heaven and the earth." However, we know now that the social system has been completely destroyed once before Adam and partially again with the flood of Noah. The destruction of the social system before Adam/pre-adamite period required a completely new social system with Adam, but following the flood of Noah, his family was allowed to restart the social system.

(See Matthew 13:35)

Verse 9 The woman here is the same subject referred to as the *great whore* in verse 1. We determined then that this is a religious system. We are told here that seven kingdoms will be affected by this religious system.

Verse 10 We are told there are seven kings. We know that kings are the head of kingdoms. The five kingdoms that have already fallen are Egypt, Assyria, Babylon, Medo-Persia, and Greece.

"And one is" in this verse is referring to the old Roman Empire. It was the Roman Empire that ruled during the time of Jesus and is currently ruling at the time John is writing the Book of Revelation.

"The other is not yet come" in this verse is referring to the seventh kingdom which is the *revised* Roman Empire because it will consist of 10 kingdoms within the old Roman Empire territory. This is why it is not referred to as the revived Roman Empire. This will occur during the last 3 ½ years of the tribulation, also known as the middle of Daniel's 70th week. This is why this scripture says "the other is not yet come; and when he cometh, he must continue a short space." Three and half years is a short space for any kingdom!!!

Verse 11 Is telling us that the Antichrist will rule the eighth kingdom and he will control the seven kingdoms and the Antichrist is the same one who will be sentenced to hell or perdition.

Verse 12 Here, John is seeing into the future. The 10 horns are 10 kings who have not been appointed kingdoms during John's time. However, they will have kingdoms during the tribulation and the time of the Antichrist.

Verse 13 is telling us that these 10 kings will give their kingdoms over to the Antichrist.

Verse 14 This is referring to the future battle of Armageddon. Jesus Christ against the Antichrist. We all know the outcome, but we are told here *the Lamb shall overcome them*.

Verse 15 This clearly explains verse 1. The waters represent a large number of people of different languages and nations. We know that the whore is a religious system that will affect all of these people.

Verse 16 This is the middle of Daniel's 70th week. The Antichrist has come into power and people are required to worship the Antichrist statue and receive his mark.

We are told that now the religious system/the whore cannot compete with Antichrist worship. So, this verse is telling us that the Antichrist and those who follow him will do away with the whore/religious system.

Verse 17 The 10 kings agree and give their kingdoms over to the Antichrist. We also Read here that this is the will of God. See God is still in charge even to the end.

Verse 18 is telling us that the woman is a great city. Remember much of what is happening during the tribulation is the fulfillment of Old Testament prophecy. With this in mind, much of the fulfillment is revealed according to biblical customs. One of those customs was that religious customs were usually centered on a city. For example, the

Jews were required to travel to Jerusalem once a year to present sacrifices and worship God.

Pagan worship was no different. An example of this can be found in Acts 19. Briefly here, Paul is in Ephesus where the people worship the idol "Diana." There is an uproar against Paul. Still, Paul eventually starts a church in Ephesus which is where we get the book of Ephesians in the bible.

Now back to Revelation 17:18. I said all that to help explain that the Antichrist came on the scene at the beginning of the tribulation, but he does not take over the temple of God until the latter half of the tribulation. The Antichrist was likely headquartered in this city where the woman/religious system was centered. It was this religious system which influenced the kings of the earth until they gave their kingdoms over to the Antichrist the last 3 ½ years of the tribulation. Notice in verse 16, the whore will be made *desolate* and they will *burn her with fire.* That is descriptive of destroying a city.

CHAPTER **18**

Verse 1 *After these things* meaning that whatever is about to happen occurred following the events of Revelation 17. Another angel comes on the scene having great power so much so that the *earth was lightened with his glory.*

This is not one of the seven angels having the seven plagues because according to Revelation 15:6, those seven angels were *clothed in pure and white linen.* The same dress that Jesus promised for the redeemed in Revelation 3:5.

Verse 2 This verse is talking about the literal city of Babylon and not just the religious system. It appears that this city had become the center of demonic operations following the rapture.

Verse 3 The city of Babylon had become a commercial center. We know that even today, the rich become addicted to wealth and are always looking for a way to get richer.

Verses 4 Another voice from heaven is calling the people of God out of Babylon to avoid the plagues of God. The wording here, *come out of her, my people* make it clear here that one of the God heads is speaking. Notice this is not the first time God has required his people to leave a sinful city to avoid God's wrath.

Genesis 19:1–26

This is in regard to the destruction of Sodom and Gomorrah. In this case, God separated his people from these cities all four of them. I want to point out a few things in these 26 verses.

1. Verse 1 clearly tells us that two angels came to Sodom but notice in verse 5 the men of the city ask, "Where are the men which came into thee this night."

Following verse 1, these angels are referred to as men in the remaining scriptures. These angels even ate like men of flesh. This reminds me of Hebrews 13:2, Read

It is apparent that Lot could see what the other men of the city could not see. The men of Sodom saw just men, but Lot saw angels.

Verse 5 Because this verse is a continuation of verse 4 and God is mentioned in this verse it is fair to assume that God the Father is not talking. Even though it is not red lettered, it is likely Jesus Christ saying "my people" in the previous verse. We have to be careful not to place too much emphasis on Jesus' words always being in red letters, especially in the Book of Revelations. The red-letter print was man's idea not the idea of Jesus; therefore, man could have missed some places. We do know, and I believe we can agree that an angel of God has never referred to God's people as "my people."

Verses 6–7 Here God has personified this city called Babylon as a queen. Keep in mind the church has gone in the rapture. The sin is so terrible in Babylon that God has called those out who are saved during the great tribulation. God is preparing to double down on his wrath on Babylon.

Verse 8 The destruction of Babylon will be swift. Three occurrences will happen on the same day. There will be death, mourning, and famine all in the same day. The mention of it being burned with fire confirms that this is the city of Babylon (or a city representing the sinful nature of Babylon of old) and not a religious system. Imagine all of this happening in one day and people not even having the time to bury their dead. Again, comparing this judgment to that of Sodom and Gomorrah in Genesis 19:1–26. These cities were burned by fire from the Lord.

Verses 9–10 These verses are proof that the religious system spoke of in Revelation 17:12–17 is different than the city being destroyed in these verses.

Here, the kings of the earth mourn over the loss of the city of Babylon because it made them all wealthy and the smoke was actually seen by the kings.

In Revelation 17:12–17, these kings will willingly give their power over to the Antichrist who is referred to as the beast in those scriptures. The Antichrist will use that power to destroy the religious system, referred to as the Mystery Babylon in, Revelation 17:5, which was set up during the tribulation.

Notice in Revelation 17:16–17, these kings agree on destroying the religious system and there is no mourning. However, when the wealthy city of Babylon is destroyed in Revelation 18:9 these same Kings "Lament for her" which is a form of mourning.

Verses 11–13 This tells us why the merchants are mourning over the loss of the city of Babylon. These are just some of the merchandise that made the merchants wealthy like gold, silver, pearls, fine linen, ivory vessels, brass, iron, marble, odors, ointments, and livestock. It appears that greed will be commonplace during the tribulation and notice also that slaves were brought back to market in the tribulation.

Verse 14 At the very end of verse 13 and here in verse 14 the soul of men is mentioned.

This verse begins with the fruits that thy soul lusted after are departed from thee. So, what is the soul of man?

1 Thessalonians 5:23

Here the spirit, soul, and body are mentioned. The body houses the spirit and soul. The spirit and body most of us understand, but what is the soul?

The word *soul* in the New Testament is translated from the Greek word *psuche*. This Greek word refers to the seat of desires, feelings, passions, appetites, and emotions. You could sum the soul up in three words: *mind, will, and emotions*. The soul controls your destiny for eternity.

An example of the distinguishing of a soul and a soul determining destiny for eternity is a wealthy Christian and a wealthy nonbeliever have very different desires, passions, and feelings about their wealth. Jesus explained it in scripture like this, "It is easier for a camel to go through the eye of a needle, than for a rich man to enter into the kingdom of God (Mark 10:25)." One big difference is that a Christian, a believer, and accepter of salvation, understands the source of his/her wealth. A nonbeliever, or rejecter of Jesus' sacrifice, will not understand the source of his/her wealth.

Now understand wealth is not the problem according to scriptures like Psalm 49:6; 49:10; 112:3. Proverbs 13:11; and Ecclesiastes 5:19.

Proverbs 13:22

This scripture makes it clear that God is not against wealth. It is telling us a Godly man will leave an inheritance to his grandchildren, but an ungodly man's wealth will be transferred to the righteous.

Your body and spirit may be separated in the end, but the soul can only be distinguished. We know you by your soul (mind, will, and emotions). Your soul will go where your spirit goes to spend eternity.

Matthew 16:26; Mark 8:36; Luke 9:25. These verses talk about a man gaining the world and losing his soul.

Verse 15–19 It is evident that these merchants are looking at a city being destroyed. This city enriched the three parts of their economy:

1. Governmental (18:9–10): The kings represent the government.

2. Commercial (18:11–16): The merchants represent sell and retail.

3. Maritime (18:17–18): Ships and sailors represent trading by sea.

Governmental because *the Kings lived deliciously* off of Babylon.

Commercial because the merchants were made wealthy by the selling and buying of gold, silver, precious stones, pearls, fine linen, ivory, brass, iron, marble, ointments, wine, oil, fine flour, wheat, livestock, chariots, and even slaves. Thirty articles of commerce total in the scriptures.

Maritime or shipping by sea was the merchant's means of distribution so the shipmasters and sailors were made wealthy also.

All of these people are mourning over the loss of their livelihood.

Verse 20 The angels in heaven are rejoicing with the holy apostles and prophets over the destruction of the city of Babylon.

Heaven is told three times in Revelation to rejoice:

1. When Satan is cast out (12:12)

2. When the city of Babylon is destroyed (18:20)

3. When the marriage of the Lamb has come, and His wife is Ready (19:7)

Verse 21 is speaking of this destruction being the final destruction of Babylon. This is also prophesied in Isaiah.

Isaiah 13:19–22

Here, Isaiah is prophesying about the final destruction of Babylon. Isaiah is comparing the destruction of Babylon with Sodom and Gomorrah and when we Read Revelation 18:10, 18, we see the similarity in the destruction. Additionally, the destruction of Sodom and Gomorrah was sudden and complete as will be the final destruction of Babylon.

Verse 22 What we are Reading here is the final day and hours of the city of Babylon. The words *no more and any more* in this verse makes it very clear that Babylon will not return as it has in the past.

Verse 23 That word *sorceries* in this verse suggest that demonic influence was found in the city of Babylon. Revelation 18:2 makes this clear.

For a better understanding of the word *sorceries,* let's go to:

Isaiah 47:12–13

In these verses, *sorceries* is better explained as enchantments, astrologers, stargazers, and monthly prognosticators. Let me define these terms for us:

1. Enchantments—a feeling of being attracted by something interesting or pretty, a quality that attracts and holds your attention. (Las Vegas is a present example of this. It is one of few places in the United States where prostitution is legal. Also, the pictures you see of Las Vegas are attractive, but these pictures do not always show you the street level.)

2. Astrology—the study of how the positions of the stars and movements of the planets have a supposed influence on events and on the lives and behavior of people. (I would venture to say that most people

know their zodiac sign. There are people today who live by and according to their zodiac sign.)

3. Stargazers—is just that, a person who gazes at the stars. This might be someone who will not make a decision unless the planets are aligned exactly right.

4. Prognosticators—to foretell from signs or symptoms.

God uses prophecy to prepare his people for what is to come. The Book of Revelations is a book of prophecy, God making his people aware of what is to come.

We can see here that sorceries and prophecy are not the same. The examples of sorceries given in Isaiah 47:12–13 are not of God but man's carnal copy of prophecy.

Verse 24 This is the end of 21 consecutive events during Daniel's 70th week, the seven seals, seven trumpets, and seven vials, beginning in Revelation Chapters 6–18.

There were other events to occur that were not in the seals, the trumpets, or the vials. One, for example, was the seven last plagues Revelation 15:6–7. Notice here that the plagues were obtained in the temple, but the seven vials of wrath were given outside the temple.

Also, notice that the city of Babylon was responsible for the death and martyrdom of many prophets and saints.

CHAPTER 19

Verse 1 John could hear a great voice of many people singing praises and giving glory and honor to the *Lord our God.* These people are the redeemed church that was raptured prior to the tribulation and some during the tribulation. We know this because of what is said in verse 8, Read. These are the saints. Again, to be a saint you have to have lived on earth. Saints were not created in heaven as the angels were. Also, John is very clear here when he says he heard people, not angels. In any case, this verse also tells us these people are *in heaven.* These people are the redeemed praising God in heaven.

Verse 2–3 These verses solidify the fact that the city of Babylon is no more. I believe this judgment was executed by

149

the Lord Jesus Christ because it is similar to the judgment executed on Sodom and Gomorrah, Jude 7, Read. The Lord judged these two cities (Genesis 18:16–33).

There are two things that Jesus made clear in the scripture when He walked the earth:

1. God the Father only knows the time of the end, Matthew 24:36, Mark 13:32.

2. Judgment would be executed by the Lord Jesus Christ, John 5:22.

Jesus is talking in those scriptures.

Verse 4 Here are the 24 elders with the 4 beasts bowing down and worshiping God.

Revelation 4:4

These are the same 24 elders. I want to point out two things here:

1. They are seated around the throne of God, which we know now is in the temple of God in heaven.

2. They are clothed in white raiment as Jesus promised the church in Revelation 3:5. The clothing of the redeemed.

Revelation 4:7–8

These are the same beasts mentioned here. The word beast here was translated from the Greek word *Zoa which means living ones or creatures*.

Verse 5 (Revelation 19) In this verse are the words small and great for a command that the redeemed and angels worship God together. We were made a little lower than the angels.

Hebrew 2:6–9

We are told here in verses 6 and 7 that man was made a little lower than the angels. In verse 9, we are told that Jesus was also made a little lower than the angels but only until His earthly death. Jesus is no longer lower than the angels. In any case, this should explain the phrase *both small and great* mentioned in Revelation 19:5.

Also, the word *fear* here does not suggest that we should actually be afraid of God. Instead, it means we should reverence God.

Verse 6 This great multitude is responding to verse 5 with praise. The word *omnipotent—means to have complete or unlimited power.*

Luke 1:37, "For with God nothing shall be impossible."

That verse explains *omnipotent power!!!*

Verse 7 Is a continuation of verse 6 where the great

multitudes are worshiping God. The reason they are worshiping is because the church and the Lord Jesus Christ are about to come together. We, the church, have been separated from the lover of the church, Jesus Christ, for ages. The coming together here is described as a marriage. Notice what is said in:

Ephesians 5:25, "Husbands, love your wives, even as Christ also loved the church, and gave himself for it."
We see that the union of a husband and wife is compared to Jesus Christ's relationship with the church.

Verse 8 Tell us who the wife of Christ is. Notice what the wife is wearing. It is the church made up of overcomers as described in Revelation 3:5, made up of saints. Remember to be a saint in heaven a person had to have lived on the earth. Saints were not created in heaven as the angels and, therefore, saints required redemption.

Verse 9 The marriage supper is a very important event in heaven and blessed are those who are called. It is not clear what the word supper is in reference to, but as believers, overcomers, now saints in heaven evidenced by the wearing of fine white linen in Verse 8, you were called while on the earth.

Romans 1:7; 1 Thessalonians 2:12; 2 Thessalonians 2:14; 1 Peter 1:15; 1 Peter 5:10.

There is no calling after death. The way you lie down in death is the way you will raise up in the end. Ecclesiastes 9:10, Read.

Verse 10 John wants to worship this angel but is told not to worship this angel. This angel called himself two things:

1. A fellow servant interpreted means equal to in status.
2. A brethren that has the testimony of Jesus Christ.

154

This angel was telling John that he is a redeemed man saved by Jesus Christ. Those of us who are saved that is our testimony.

This scene began in Revelation 17:1 with one of the seven angels in Revelation 15:6 calling John up to show him *the judgment of the great whore*. Remember how that angel is *clothed in pure and white linen* in Revelation 15:6. Jesus said in Revelation 3:5 *he that overcometh, the same shall be clothed in white raiment*. Notice this was said to the church.

Verse 11–13 We group these three scriptures together because in them is the identity of the one sitting on this white horse. His identity can be no clearer than in verse 13 *his name is called The Word of God*. This is Jesus Christ on this white horse!!!

John 1:1, 14

"[1]In the beginning was the Word, and the Word was with God, and the Word was God. [14]And the Word was made flesh, and dwelt among us, (and we beheld his glory, the glory as of the only begotten of the Father,) full of grace and truth."

We know Jesus is the only one who came from heaven to earth in the flesh. There have been many prophets who have walked the earth, but they did not originate in heaven. Jesus originated in heaven and walked on earth.

We do want to remember that the Antichrist also is described to be sitting on a white horse in Revelation 6:1–2. First, keep in mind that the Antichrist is an imitator of Jesus Christ. Also, in these scriptures, the "Lamb" (Jesus) releases the Antichrist from the first of seven seals.

Revelation 19:14 Again notice the army with Jesus following him from heaven on white horses. Notice their dress *clothed in fine linen, white and clean.* This army is the redeemed church as described in Revelation 3:5.

Verse 15 Here, Jesus is described as having a sharp sword that comes forth from his mouth. With this, Jesus will smite the nations.

Hebrews 4:12

This same word of God is our weapon as we walk out this salvation. Also, notice how the word *is a discerner of the thoughts and intents of the heart.*

John 18:6, "As soon then as he had said unto them, I am he, they went backward, and fell to the ground."

I would encourage you to Read the previous scriptures, but this was just a small demonstration of the power that comes forth from the mouth of Jesus when He speaks.

Verse 16 The He in this verse is Jesus. We know this because Jesus is the only *King of Kings and Lord of Lords.* This simply means that Jesus is the highest of the highest. This name is written on His thigh (leg) and *vesture.*

Now a thigh is flesh. I can visualize a tattoo. I have got nothing against a tattoo but if I was to get a tattoo, it would need to be something of great significance.

Vesture—a covering garment (as a robe); something that covers like a garment.

Verses 17–18 Remember a description of the nation's being slain was in verse 15. Now with all the dead flesh, the fowls of the air are summoned to the ground to eat. References are made to the battle of *Armageddon* even though it is not mentioned in these verses. *Armageddon is mentioned once in Revelation 16:16.*

The small and great mentioned in verse 18 plainly tell us it is referring to men in the battle of Armageddon on the earth. This is not the same as the small and great mentioned in verse 5 for two reasons:

1. These are in heaven
2. It includes all servants and those who fear or reverence God

This verse includes all angels and all the redeemed in heaven because we all are servants of God and we all fear or reverence God.

Verse 19 This verse is talking about two opposing armies. The beast mentioned is the antichrist along with the kings of the earth and their armies. They are gathered together to war against him that sat on the horse and his army.

The one sitting on the horse is the same one mentioned in Revelation 19:11–16. He is our Lord Jesus Christ from heaven with his army from heaven.

Two very distinct differences in these two armies are that the army of the beast and the kings of the earth are from earth. The army of the King of Kings and Lord of Lords is from heaven (Revelation 19:14).

Verse 20 The Antichrist and the false prophet both were cast alive into the lake of fire and brimstone. Notice their punishment did not include a natural death. Also, there is no coming back from the lake of fire burning with brimstone. That is the final judgment and stop for anyone who rejects the Lord Jesus Christ.

Verse 21 Announces a victory for the Lord and his army. We are the Lord's army (Revelation 19:14) *clothed in fine linen, white, and clean.* Notice something else in verse 21, there are no slain or casualties in the Lord's army, but the opposing armies are slain. We the redeemed will be there but the battle is the Lord's.

This is the battle at Armageddon spoke of in Revelation 16:16.

CHAPTER **20**

Verse 1 The bottomless pit is not the hell following judgment but a place of restraint. The hell following judgment is where the lake of fire and brimstone is located.

So, whether it is the bottomless pit or the lake of fire and brimstone both represent a separation from God.

Notice this angel had a key and *a great chain in his hand.*

2 Peter 2:4

These are angels cast down to hell where they are detained in chains until the Day of Judgment. Hell is used here to signify separation from God.

Verse 2 The dragon here is referred to by three other names serpent, Devil, and Satan. The dragon will be bound in that chain mentioned in verse 1 for a thousand years.

162

Verse 3 The dragon will be cast into the bottomless pit and shut up. Remember the angel in verse 1 had a key, so we would be correct in saying the dragon was locked up in the bottomless pit.

The word *bottomless* is translated from the Greek word *abussos* which means unfathomed, enormous, abyss, unbounded (without boundary), and immeasurable depth.

Additionally, a seal will be set upon him. Remember the Antichrist was released in Revelation 6:1–2 by the first seal Jesus opened. However, the Antichrist did not come out of the bottomless pit because the bottomless pit is first mentioned in Revelation 9:1.

We know that the bottomless pit itself is a place of restraint so why add the seal over the dragon?

Answer: It appears that the bottomless pit will restrain the movement of the dragon, but the seal prevents the dragon from acting or having influence.

Notice the dragon was first shut up in verse 3 and then a seal was *set upon him that he should deceive the nations no more.* With this in mind, the rapture could come in our lifetime!!! The following explains the possibility of the Antichrist living at any time.

See it is possible that the Antichrist could be living right now but the seal on him, mentioned in Revelation 6:1–2, is preventing the Antichrist from acting or having influence before the rapture. Just like the seal on Satan mentioned in Revelation 20:3 will prevent him from deceiving the nations during the 1000 years millennium.

Again, the rapture could come at any time!!! Those of us who go with the rapture will be looking down from heaven when the seal is removed from the Antichrist.

Jesus will reign with the saints on the earth a thousand years. After a thousand years, Satan will be loosed on the earth again for a little season. The phrase *a little season* is not clearly defined.

2nd Peter 3:8, "But, beloved be not ignorant of this one thing, that one day is with the Lord as a thousand years and a thousand years as one day."

So, a little season is what the Lord determines it to be.

Verse 4 In this verse, the millennium or thousand-year reign or rule of Jesus Christ begins on earth. Those who are saints are with Jesus. The word *thrones* could be interpreted as seats. Apparently, it is clear here that we will not be standing for a thousand years.

Mark 10:35–40

Here, the disciples James and John, brothers, request to sit on Jesus' right and left. However, they are told in verse 40, by Jesus in effect, that those seats are reserved already.

Jesus' reign on earth was prophesied to the Jews for centuries. So, when Jesus came to earth for the first time they were expecting Jesus to set up his kingdom then. When it did not happen, the Jews rejected Jesus as the Messiah and crucified him. The crucifixion of Jesus opened up the door of salvation for non-Jews like us. If you are not a Jew, you are a Gentile.

Those who refused to worship the beast or his image and refused to receive the mark were beheaded for their refusal. We are told here *they lived and reigned with Christ a thousand years.*

These are people in the tribulation. Repentance for them came by simply (not so simple if you are there) refusing the beast. This proved to be enough to be accepted by the Lord Jesus Christ. Another way to say it is "their witness for Jesus Christ as Lord and Savior was seen in their refusal" which resulted in their death. *After all, trading your life for Christ is the most anyone can do for Christ.*

Verse 5 The first resurrection is complete. All of the righteous have been raptured or resurrected. Only the resurrection of the wicked remains to be done and this will not happen until after the thousand-year millennium is finished.

Verse 6 Blessed and holy are those who have been a part of the first resurrection. We will be priests of God and Christ during the thousand years.

Verse 7 remember Satan was secured and a seal placed on him in the bottomless pit in verses 2–3 of this chapter. Now, he will be loosed out of his prison. This prison was called a *bottomless pit* in Revelation 20:3. Just like I explained following verse 3, the bottomless pit is not the same as the lake of fire and brimstone where the Antichrist and the false prophet were cast into in Revelation 19:20.

Verse 8 The battle of Armageddon has already happened at this time a thousand years earlier. The army of the Antichrist was defeated in Revelation 19:20–21 and he and the false prophet *both were cast alive into a lake of fire burning with brimstone.*

Satan was loosed from prison in Revelation 20:7. The land of Gog and Magog is found north of Palestine in Asia. This could include nations that we know today as Persia (the territories of Iran and Iraq), Ethiopia, and Libya (Ezekiel 38:5).

Satan has found many on the earth still, who are not saints, to follow him. Apparently, there are nations on the earth who have not wanted the reign of Christ and have longed in their hearts to eliminate the rigid suppression of their lusts.

1 Chronicles 5:3–4

Here, the first time Gog is mentioned in the Bible, we discover that he was a descendant of Reuben, the firstborn of Jacob/Israel. Now understand the Gog mentioned here is not the same person in Revelations but because the scriptures are inspired by God, who knows all, the Gog mentioned in Revelations represents the rebellion that almighty God knew would come from the Old Testament Gog.

Ezekiel 38:2, 14–18

First of all, we know from verse 2 that Gog is the leader of the people of Magog. Beginning in verse 14, Ezekiel is told by God to prophesy against Gog. Gog will lead an army against God's *people of Israel* in the latter days. God's fury or anger will rise up.

Ezekiel 39:6

This is a prophecy of the final battle mentioned in Revelation 20:9. We know this because, in the battle of Armageddon before the 1000-year millennium, the army against the Lord was destroyed by the sword that proceeded out of the mouth of the Lord (Revelation 19:21). Fire was not used. Additionally, Jesus fought the battle at Armageddon. God will fight the final battle with fire (Revelation 20:9).

Gog here represents a spirit of antichrist. We know the Antichrist was not around for the destruction by fire because the Antichrist was cast into the lake of fire following the battle of Armageddon (Revelation 19:20).

Remember Satan is the leader of this army. So, the Gog mentioned in Revelation 20:8 is representative of the rebellious sin nature of the nations who follow Satan to come against the New Jerusalem after the 1000-year millennium.

Verse 9 These people who we can now refer to as rebels gather with Satan and surround the saints and the capital New Jerusalem where Jesus rules.

Now, notice God the Father has had enough and fire is rained down from heaven and devour them. Jesus did not have to fight this battle. I believe that this happened so quickly that the reign of Jesus was not even interrupted.

Verse 10 Following this defeat, the devil is cast into the lake of fire where the Antichrist and the false prophet were cast into in Revelation 19:20. There is no coming back from the lake of fire and brimstone and there is *torment day and night forever and ever.* Forever and ever is the same as eternity.

Verse 11 The judgment of the second resurrection is about to occur. The saints and those of the first resurrection will not be judged because they have already been in heaven with Jesus and have lived with Jesus on earth during the reign of Jesus in the millennium. Just like there is no coming back from the lake of fire and brimstone, there is also no coming back from heaven.

What is apparent to me is that those who were destroyed by fire in Revelation 20:8–9 had never been to heaven. According to verse 3, there are people, other than those defeated at Armageddon, still on the earth when Jesus comes with the saints to start the thousand-year reign. We know this because verse 3 Reads the devil would not deceive the *nations* until the thousand-year reign of Jesus is concluded. Nations is the key word there because it is not referring to those with Jesus who came from heaven and accompanied Jesus at Armageddon. Even without the influence of Satan during the thousand-year reign of Jesus, they still do not accept Jesus as Lord and Savior. These people are truly lost!

The mercy of God is in action to the very end. Psalm 100:5; Psalm 106:1; Psalm 107:1; Psalm 118:2–4; Psalm 136:2–26. There are more scriptures that declare the mercy of God.

He who is sitting on the *great white throne* is Jesus. We know this because God the Father has designated Jesus as the judge.

John 5:22, "For the Father judgeth no man, but hath committed all judgment unto the Son."

The words *earth and the heaven fled away* are used in a figurative sense here. We know this because the earth was created eternal.

Psalm 78:69; 104:5; Ecclesiastes 1:4

More explanation regarding the topic of the earth being eternal will be revealed in the first verse of Revelation 21:1.

Verse 12 This is the second resurrection, the resurrection of the wicked. Notice two different categories of books were opened: the *books* and *the book of life*. The wicked were judged *out of those things which were written in the books, according to their works.* The *book of life* has the names of the righteous written in it.

We know the righteous will not be judged because the righteous have already been to heaven following the first resurrection and have spent 1000 years under the reign of Jesus.

Revelation 3:5

Jesus is talking here. The overcomers are clothed in white raiment (clothing, garments, etc.) and their names are written in the book of life.

Psalm 69:28

David is praying here that there be a separation, in the book of life, of the wicked from the righteous.

Exodus 32:32

Moses knew there was a book which separated the wicked from the righteous.

Verse 13 The lost dead are retrieved from three places:

The sea, death, and hell.

The sea represents the unburied dead. Maritime law allows for dead bodies to be thrown overboard, commonly referred to as being buried at sea.

Death refers to the bodies of those who have died, whose bodies have decayed into dust.

Hell, here is translated from the Greek word *Hades,* which is the intermediate residence for lost spirits. Because the righteous spirit when absent from the body immediately go to be with the Lord (2 Corinthians 5:6–8) so there had to be a place for the unrighteous spirit to go and Hades is that place.

Revelation 20:4 is a very good example of 2 Corinthians 5:8 being fulfilled were those who had not worshiped the beast (Antichrist), neither his image, neither had received his mark upon their foreheads, nor in their hands are alive and reigning with Christ a thousand years.

However, there are other places in scripture where the Greek word *Gehenna* is translated *hell,* an example of that is found in Luke 12:5. The Greek word *Gehenna* is translated to the word *hell* here to mean the same as the lake of fire.

In any case, no one will escape the judgment. Remember this is the resurrection of the wicked only. The righteous are already with the Lord and are not being judged.

Verse 14 Death and hell here refers to everyone whose body has been dead until the second resurrection. Their wick spirits were not with Christ. Their spirits were held in hades/hell, the holding place for unrepentant spirits. These are people who did not accept Jesus Christ as Lord and Savior during their lifetime on earth, which if you remember is the only opportunity a person has to become a saint.

Verse 15 Only those who accepted the salvation offered through the sacrifice of our Lord and Savior Jesus Christ on the cross of Calvary will find their names written in the book of life.

Those who reject Jesus Christ will not find their names written in the book of life. Those people will be cast into the lake of fire. There is no returning from the lake of fire.

CHAPTER 21

Verse 1 A new heaven and a new earth really means a renovated heavens and earth, the atmospheric heavens not the residence heaven of God. The phrase *passed away* was translated from the Greek word *parerchomai* which means pass from one condition to another. This is not an annihilation of earth. As we go forward, please remember as I have said many times, "No scripture voids, disqualifies, or cancels out another scripture because all scriptures are truth." This is why the scripture tells us that the Holy Spirit will teach us all truth (John 16:13; John 15:26).

2 Peter 3:10–12

These verses are speaking about the same space in time as Revelation 21:1. We know this because it mentions *the day of the Lord* or interpreted *the coming of the Lord.*

Heavens mentioned here is referring to the atmospheric heavens, not the residential heaven.

Elements mentioned here are translated from the Greek word *stoicheion.* It has references to the principals or basic elements of the present world system which consist of evil spirits, a sinful and fallen nature, disease, germs, corruptions, and all elements by which men corrupt themselves.

Understand that the sin of man, which includes greed, has created certain atmospheric problems that cannot be seen with the naked eye; like pollution—we breathe it in every day, affecting our health. I cannot imagine my Lord living and breathing what we breathe every day, especially since He has the power to change it. So, the heavens or atmosphere will be changed.

Keep in mind, there has never been any sin in God's residential heaven, so there is no need to destroy God's residence. Additionally, the scripture tells us that the earth is established forever.

Psalms 78:69

The "He" in that verse is God. This verse is comparing the sanctuary of God to the earth *which he has established forever.* So, a correct interpretation of this scripture would be that both the sanctuary of God and the earth are established forever.

Other scriptures explaining that the earth is forever are found in Psalm 104:5; 119:90; Ecclesiastes 1:4.

There have been two previous times when God could have destroyed the earth and He did not. The first time was in Genesis 1:2, the first flood brought on at the end of the Preadamite period. The second was during the flood of Noah's time.

Genesis 1:31, "And God saw everything that he had made, and, behold, it was very good, and the evening and the morning were the sixth day."

Was God wrong? Or was everything God made *very good.* Just food for thought.

Revelation 21:1 No more sea does not mean that there will not be any more water on earth. I located a number of scriptures which speak of a river running from the sanctuary of God (Ezekiel 47) during the millennial. No more sea is suggesting that there won't be any larger oceans.

Verse 2 The New Jerusalem comes down from God out of heaven prepared as a bride adorned for her husband. Notice the city is prepared as a bride adorned for her husband. The word "AS" in this scripture is very important because this means the city is being *compared* to a bride. We see how the Holy City is Adorned in Revelation 21:19.

The word *bride* in this scripture is translated from the Greek word *numphe*. This Greek word has also been used to mean daughter-in-law in Matthew 10:35; Luke 12:53, and wife in Revelation 19:7. In any case, a bride is prepared to be married and a daughter-in-law and wife are already married. Verse 3 It has always been the plan of God to live and dwell among men.

Genesis 3:8

Here, before the curse, God is walking in the Garden of Eden where Adam and Eve are hiding. We know that they were not hid from God and I do not believe this was the first time God visited them in the Garden because the scripture said *they heard the voice of the Lord God.* So, they knew his voice. Just like the scripture does not mention how many times God had been in the Garden; the scripture also does not tell us how long Adam and Eve lived before they committed the transgression. It is very possible they lived a considerable amount of time before they ate from the tree of knowledge of good and evil. In any case, the point I wanted to make is that God walked among them in the Garden of Eden.

Verse 4 Remember what we learned about the soul of man in Revelation 18:13; the soul consists of the mind, will, and emotions. We already knew the body would be transformed but we are actually being told here that the soul will be converted as well. We know this because sorrow and crying are emotions we currently experience under the curse. No more death because all things will become eternal. The pain is removed because you and I know that physical pain can incite emotions like tears and crying.

Verses 5–6 The "he" that sat on the throne is Alpha and Omega. We know this to be Jesus Christ because of Revelation 1:8, 11.

I believe Jesus said these words in Revelation 21:6. I have a red-letter edition Bible, yet these words are not red lettered. Just another reason we should not get caught up in red letters being the only time Jesus spoke.

"It is done" mentioned in verse 6 is referring to the will of God having been fulfilled.

Like it was explained earlier, making all things new does not mean that everything will be recreated but instead the curse will be removed from all things. Removing the curse will bring about a renewal of heaven and earth not a recreation.

Verse 7 This is still Jesus talking, a continuation of verses 5–6. To understand what Jesus is saying and why Jesus is saying it, we need to Read Revelation 3:5 (Read). There Jesus was referring to the church. The overcomers dressed in white raiment are the church. We are the church. Jesus is Lord and God over us, the church.

Ephesians 1:20–22

We know the trinity does exist still verse 22 tells us that God the Father has given Jesus *to be head over all things to the church.* Interpreted this makes Jesus Lord over us because we are the church.

Revelation 21:8 There are eight kinds of people listed here who will split eternal hell wide open:

1. The fearful—is translated from the Greek word *deilos* which means cowardly, craven, vile, worthless, miserable, wretched, and unhappy.

2. Unbelieving—is translated from the Greek word *apistos* which means infidel and faithless (1 Timothy 5:8).

3. Abominable—is translated from the Greek word *bdelusso* which means to cause to stink, make loathsome, feel disgusted, detest, have horror of, to be abominated. It refers to those polluted with unnatural lust.

4. Murderers—is translated from the Greek word *phoneus* which is only translated, murderer.

5. Whoremongers—is translated from the Greek word *pornois* which refers to fornication.

6. Sorcerers—is translated from the Greek word *pharmakeusin* which refers to persons who by use of drugs, enchanted potions, charms, and enchantments seek to produce supernatural effects in the lives of others.

7. Idolaters—those who practice idolatry and abominable immoral acts in the worship of idols.

8. Liars—is an English word, no interpretation needed.

Romans 6:23

This is one of the most preached scriptures of the Bible, but after hearing this, many people continue their lifestyle of sin because death is not immediate and the scripture in Hebrew 11:25 tells us there are pleasures in sin but only for a season followed by the wages. The following is an explanation of that word death.

We were created to be with God when sin causes us to be separated from God that is death to our spirit. Death, in this case, does not mean that the spirit dies because we know the spirit is eternal. These sins mentioned in Revelation 21:8 are descriptive of the lives of these people while living on earth. At the death of their physical body, it was certain that their spirits would not be with God and so they would not have been in the first resurrection. That was the first death or separation from God.

The second death or separation from God mentioned in Revelation 21:8 is referring to the second and final time these people will be separated from God. They will be in the second resurrection. They will be cast into the lake of fire and brimstone. This is a permanent and final destination.

Revelation 21:9–10 This is referring to one of the seven angels first mentioned in Revelation 15:1, 6 with the seven last plagues and dressed in pure white linen. We determined previously that these were redeemed men who appeared to

John to be angels, possibly because they came out of the temple of God in heaven.

The bride and the Lamb's wife is the *holy Jerusalem descending out of heaven from God* the Father. Understand that a bride is imminent to marriage and a wife is married. Now referring back to Revelation 19:7–8, there is a joining together of the church which includes Jesus Christ and the New Jerusalem. This is the marriage.

Verse 11 is a description of the New Jerusalem. Notice it says having the glory of God the Father. A Jasper stone is a sea-green color.

Revelation 4:3

The throne of God is described here. To John, the glory of God looked like jasper and sardine stone which has a red appearance. So now we have sea-green and red together. Remember John is seeing this and describing it in terms he can relate to. The glory of God is probably more beautiful than any of us can imagine.

Verses 12–13, We find in these scriptures that the New Jerusalem is surrounded by a wall great (probably meaning thick) and high (meaning tall). An example of a thick wall is found in:

Joshua 2:15

This was the wall of Jericho, a wall thick enough to allow the harlot Rahab's house to be built on top of it. This was typical in biblical days when walls, built for protection, surrounded a city.

Another example similar to the one in Joshua is found in:

2 Corinthians 11:33

Paul the Apostle was let down from a window on the wall of Damascus and escaped capture. A window signifies to me there was a house on this wall as in Jericho.

Revelation 21:12-13

The New Jerusalem has 12 gates, 3 on each side. The gates are guarded by 12 angels. Written on the gates are the names of the 12 tribes of Israel. Probably the same 12 tribes mentioned in

Revelation 7:5–8, Read. This is the most recent list. If you Read the names from the Old Testament list, you will find there were some changes.

Verse 14 The wall has 12 foundations. Each foundation has the name of the 12 apostles of the Lamb, Jesus Christ. The apostles were previously the 12 disciples of Jesus while

Jesus lived. Now, remember Judas Iscariot hung himself as a disciple. The disciples were not called apostles in the bible until Jesus died, rose, and ascended into heaven. So, Matthias, the replacement for Judas Iscariot, will be the twelfth name on the wall's foundation (Acts 1:26).

Verse 15 The He in this verse is still one of the seven angels. A measuring reed was about 12 ½ feet long. Unlike the measuring reed found in Revelation 11:1, this reed was golden. This reed is compared to a rod in Revelation 11:1.

Verse 16 We are told that the city is a perfect square in length, width (breadth), and height. Twelve thousand furlongs is equal to 1500 square miles. The angel/redeemed man is doing all the measuring.
Furlong—a unit of distance equal to 220 yards (about 201.2 meters) or 1/8 of a mile.

Let's try some basic math. There are 528 feet in 1/10 of a mile and there is 10/10 of a mile in one mile. So, 528 feet multiplied by 10 equals 5280 feet in one mile.

There are 3 feet to a yard and a furlong is 220 yards, 220 multiplied by 3 equals 660 feet in a furlong. Multiply 660 feet (a furlong) by 12,000 feet and you get 7,920,000 feet. Now divide 7,920,000 feet by 5280 feet (equivalent to a mile) and you get 1500 miles.

Verse 17 A cubit is approximately 18 inches, the distance from the elbow to the tip of the middle finger known as the forearm. I took this measurement of my forearm and it was approximately 20 inches. So, this measurement could vary on each of us.

The note in my bible has a cubit at 25 inches, making the wall 300 feet tall. This would make each cubit 2 feet and 1 inch. Multiplying 144 cubits by 2 feet each and you get 288 feet, this still leaves 12 feet unaccounted for.

We need to add the inch to each of the 144 cubits, 144 inches divided by 12 inches equals 12 feet. 288 feet plus 12 feet will get us 300 feet.

Please keep in mind the notes in any of our Bibles are not scripture but do serve as a guide to give us an idea of the height of the wall of New Jerusalem.

Again, one of the seven angels is doing the measurements using measuring terms that were relevant in John's day.

Verse 18 Jasper—is a blackish green. This is the making of the wall and the New Jerusalem is pure gold, clear as glass. Revelation 4:3

The glory of God also has the appearance of Jasper along with a sardine stone which is red in color.

Revelation 21:19–20

The New Jerusalem has 12 foundations, each made of a different precious stone.

1. Jasper—a blackish green (dark green)

2. Sapphire—a blue stone, next to a diamond in hardness

3. Chalcedony—a transparent stone with four known possibilities (a bluish white, a dull milky veined, a brownish black, and a yellow-red)

4. Emerald—green color

5. Sardonyx—bluish white and red

6. Sardius—bloodred stone

7. Chrysolite—a gold-like stone; a dusky green with a yellow cast

8. Beryl—a transparent gem of bluish green

9. Topaz—a pale green gem with a mixture of yellow

10. Chrysoprasus—a yellowish green stone with a bluish hue of the Chrysolite kind

11. Jacinth—a stone of red color with a mixture of yellow

12. Amethyst—a stone of purple or violet color composed of strong blue and deep red.

Many of these stones were set in the breastplate of the High Priest in Exodus 28:17–21.

Verse 21 Remember in Revelation 21:12, we are told that the *names of the 12 tribes of the children of Israel* will be written on these gates.

Each gate will be a pearl, keeping in mind that the wall will be 144 cubits high. This would imply that each gate would likely be 144 cubits high to accommodate the height of the wall. Also, we are told in verse 12 that an angel will be posted at each gate. I can only imagine that it would take the strength of an angel to control a 144-cubit high pearl gate. However according to Revelation 21:25 *the gates of it shall not be shut at all.* So the angel is not there to open or close the gate.

The streets of New Jerusalem will be pure transparent gold, like glass. Now you know where the words "streets paved with gold" come from in the songs you hear.

Verse 22 We know there is a temple in heaven, Revelation 16:17, so depending on your translation either there will not be a temple building in New Jerusalem or there will be a building but not necessary for worship because God the Father and Jesus the Lamb are always present and available for worship.

I take the scripture at its word; I believe that John saw no temple because one will not be necessary. As the scripture says God Almighty and Jesus the Lamb, two of the Trinity, will be present in New Jerusalem.

Verse 23 Certainly no need for artificial light and according to the scripture there will be no need for light from the sky in New Jerusalem.

Verse 24 It appears that New Jerusalem will not be the only population existing on the earth for eternity. There will be other nations who are saved and have earthly kings who may enter into the gates of New Jerusalem.

Verse 25 The gates will never close and there will be no night in the New Jerusalem.

Verse 26 Still proofs that there will be other populations on the earth along with the residents of New Jerusalem.

Verse 27 Notice the only survivors of eternity were those documented in the *Lambs book of life*, just as Jesus said in

Revelation 3:5. The book of life and the Lambs book of life are the same book.

Remember the angels are guarding the gates of New Jerusalem, Revelation 21:12. So as the scripture says nothing that defileth, or worketh abomination, or maketh a lie will enter into the city.

CHAPTER **22**

Verse 1 A pure and clear river of water flowing from the throne of God and of the Lamb, Jesus. Here, God the Father and Jesus share the throne. One might ask how is this possible?

Revelation 5:1–6, Read

We know that verse 1 is God the Father. In verse 6, we Read that *in the midst of the throne stood a lamb as it had been slain.* We know the Lamb is Jesus Christ.

The word Lamb here is translated from the Greek word *arnion* which is translated 27 times in Revelation to mean

Christ except Revelation 13:11, Read. This lamb is referring to the false prophet, the second beast. Notice the scriptures Read he was *like a lamb, and he spake as a dragon.* So, we know, in this case, it was not Christ because he spoke like the dragon, Satin.

Verse 2 This street is made of pure gold according to Revelation 21:21. The image I get when Reading this is a boulevard with a median in the middle and the *river of water of life, clear as crystal* (verse 1) running alongside the boulevard. The boulevard had a row of the tree of life *in the midst* (in the median) of it and the river having a row of the tree of life on each side of it. The Boulevard, river, and trees of life will run the length of the city, 1500 miles (Revelation 21:16).

The tree of life is mentioned in the singular but we know there is more than one because:

1. One is mentioned in the midst of the boulevard.

2. Two are mentioned, one on each side of the river of life.

Taking into consideration that the city will be 1500 miles square, I believe there will be rows of the tree of life along the boulevard and river. The tree of life will bare 12 different fruits and the leaves of the tree of life will heal the nations.

So, we have scripture in Revelation 21:24–26; Revelation 22:2 indicating there will be nations living outside the city of New Jerusalem. Man will be living out the original plan of God (Revelation 21:4) with no tears, death, sorrow, crying, or pain.

Genesis 3:22–24

The tree of life (likely one tree in this case) is in the Garden of Eden. Adam and Eve are sent from the Garden of Eden following their disobedience (Genesis 2:16–17; 3:6) to God by eating the fruit from the tree of the knowledge of good and evil. There was health and prosperity while Adam and Eve were obedient to God. The curse came following their disobedience. God knew that with one rebellion from Adam and Eve another would follow, and they would have eaten from the tree of life had they remained in the Garden of Eden.

Revelation 22:3 There will be no more curse. Adam and Eve's rebellion in the Garden of Eden brought on the curse. The throne of God and the Lamb will be in the New Jerusalem. Here, also the redeemed and the angels will serve him.

Verse 4 Keep in mind, we have entered into eternity at this time. The redeemed and the angels will actually see the face of God. This is significant because of what God told Moses in Exodus 33:20 (Read). This is before the judgment and wrath of God. So, if any man tells you he has seen God before the judgment, he has lied to you. However, it is possible to see or encounter Jesus because the Apostle Paul, then Saul, did meet Jesus on the road to Damascus (Acts 9:2–7).

Verse 5 The pronoun "they" in this verse is a continuation or an extension of the word *servants* in verse 3, so it is speaking of us the redeemed along with the angels. There will be no darkness in New Jerusalem. Now notice light will be provided by the *Lord God*. I will attempt to provide you an explanation about who *Lord God* is.

Ephesians 1:3–10, Read

First, I must remind you that Jesus said only God the Father knows the time of the end in Matthew 24:36; Mark 13:32.

We all know John 3:16 how God the Father loved the world so much that he gave Jesus his son for it. These verses, along with many more that are not mentioned, tell me that God the Father has been in charge from the beginning of our time (God the Father is timeless). Now with that as a foundation, I will attempt to explain Ephesians 1:3–10.

Ephesians 1:3

We clearly see here two persons of the Trinity, God the Father and our Lord Jesus Christ. This scripture is telling us that God the Father has in effect blessed *Us* with all spiritual blessings in heavenly places. Since the Apostle Paul, a man, is the writer of the book of Ephesians, we know that *Us* in that scripture is inclusive of you and I the redeemed. See how God the Father is exalted here.

Verse 4 (Ephesians)

We know that verse 3 was exalting God the Father for his plan of salvation in Jesus Christ. This verse is a continuation of that exalting by telling us that God the Father chose us before the foundation of the world to be holy and without blame. That only comes to us through Jesus Christ. In effect, this scripture is telling us that God's plan of salvation through Jesus Christ was known to God from the very beginning.

Verse 5 (Ephesians)

The word predestination in God's word does not mean that God predetermined who would not be saved. Instead, it means that God's plan to save the world through Jesus Christ was predetermined even before sin appeared on the scene. Yes, it is true that God the Father knew in Advance who would accept His plan and who would reject it, but the plan is available for everyone.

Verse 6 (Ephesians)

God the Father has brought us into his grace through his beloved Son Jesus Christ.

Verse 7 (Ephesians)

We are redeemed through the blood of Jesus Christ. With redemption comes the forgiveness of sins according to the grace of God the Father. Remember grace is an unmerited favor. So, because grace is an unmerited favor, God the Father chose the method by which we may be forgiven. Thus, he provided one way and one way only and that is by the shed blood of our Lord and Savior Jesus Christ.

Verse 8 (Ephesians)

The scripture here says in *all wisdom and* prudence because God the Father has provided us with all the wisdom, in his word, that we need to make the choice of salvation. Prudence is the practice of applying that wisdom in a timely fashion to bring about the best results.

Verse 9 (Ephesians)

The *his, he, and himself* in that verse is talking about God the Father.

Verse 10 (Ephesians)

This is a prophecy regarding the millennium, we have Read about in the book of Revelation. The millennium is where all things will be brought to Jesus Christ for 1000 years.

The word *dispensation* is translated from the Greek word *oikonomia* which means stewardship.

The English word dispensation means—permission to break a law or an official promise you have made: release from a rule, vow, or oath: an act of providing something to people.

In short, man is currently in a probationary period operating as steward over the earth until the curse is gone and God reclaims it. The curse is completely gone following the millennium as we have Read in Revelation. The fullness of times is nearer than we think.

Back to Revelation 22:5 for an explanation about the *Lord God* in that verse.

Hebrew 1:1–3, 13

We know these scriptures are talking about Jesus Christ. We are told here that Jesus *sat down on the right hand of the majesty on high* which we know is God the Father. We Read in verse 13 that this is to occur until his enemies are made his footstool. The word *until* in that verse is very important because it implies that something will change when ALL enemies are put underfoot.

1 Corinthians 15:24–26 (summary)

We learn here that death is the last enemy to be destroyed. Death is finally destroyed by God the Father in Revelation 20:9, 14. We know this because there is no more death in Chapters 21 and 22. Remember Jesus was to sit on the right hand of God the Father *until* all enemies were defeated. Now, the final enemy death is gone.

1 Corinthians 15:24–28 (explained)

After reading the Book of Revelation, we all know that the end was not when the rapture of the church from the earth occurred. Instead, the end will come following the 1000-year millennium reign of Jesus Christ on earth. Now, these scriptures are telling us what will happen at the final end.

The first He in verse 24 is Jesus delivering up the kingdom to God the Father. Jesus is going to give all rule, authority, and power to God the Father.

The first He in verse 25 is Jesus, the second He is God the Father. We know this because Jesus has reigned for 1000 years and it was God the Father who put the enemies underfoot in Revelation 20:9.

Notice the *till* in this verse and go back and Read Hebrew 1:13 again. The word *till* in 1 Corinthians 15:25 has the exact same meaning as the word *until* in Hebrew 1:13. The *his* in this verse 25 is also Jesus.

1 Corinthians 15:26 The last enemy destroyed is death. This scripture Reads in the future text because at the time of this writing the church was still on the earth; therefore, this had not occurred yet.

Verse 27 (1 Corinthians) The *he* in this verse is God the Father. The *his* and *him* in this verse is Jesus. Let's replace the pronouns with the proper nouns and Read it like this:

For God, the Father hath put all things under Jesus' feet. But when God the Father saith all things are put under Jesus, it is manifest that God the Father is excepted, which did put all things under Jesus.

Verse 28 is much clearer. All things are now subdued unto God the Father. Now, the Son (Jesus) himself is subject to God the Father who put all things under Jesus. Now, God, the Father is *all in all*!!!

In the end, the Son and Holy Spirit will come together in God the Father to reign together in eternity. Sin made it necessary for them to take separate roles in the redemption process.

Revelation 22:6 The angel talking to John is authenticating the truthfulness of the things said and shown to John.

Revelation 1:1, Read

Here, we get the total authentication. God the Father gave the revelation of Jesus Christ to Jesus Christ, and Jesus Christ gave this revelation to his angel, and his angel gave the revelation to John. So, we have four witnesses of this revelation:

1. God the Father

2. Jesus Christ

3. The angel of Jesus Christ

4. John, the writer of the Book of Revelation

Verse 7 If you have a red-letter edition bible, then you know Jesus is talking here. Let's put this word *quickly* in perspective. I have shown you in Chapter 20 how the Antichrist could be living among us at any given time, which also means that the rapture could occur at any given time followed by a seven-year tribulation. Seven years is not a long time. Most of us can remember where we were and what we were doing seven years ago.

In Revelation 1:3, we are told of the blessing that comes with reading, hearing, and keeping the words of this prophecy. Now in the very last Book of Revelation, we are practically told the same thing. It would appear that John placed this saying in the first book of Revelation to encourage the Reader, even us. Since this study began, I have heard from several people who are afraid to Read or study the book of Revelations.

Verse 8 Remember going back to Revelation 15:6 and 17:1 we know that this is one of the seven angels talking with John. We also know now that this angel is a redeemed man which is why this angel responds the way he does in verse 9.

Verse 9 this angel identifies himself as:

1. A fellow servant

2. Brethren of the prophets

3. As one of those who keep the saying of this book

Notice number 3 further reveals that this angel is a redeemed man because he is required to keep or follow this book as we are. The bible was not written for those who were created angels, but for the saints who were redeemed and became angels.

Verse 10 John is encouraged here to put what he has witnessed in a book and share it. This is why John is sometimes referred to as "John the Revelator" because it is through John that the Book of Revelations is revealed to us. In the Book of Revelation, we are told what to expect following the crucifixion of Jesus Christ beginning with:

1. The churches on earth.

2. Followed by the rapture of the church from the earth.

3. Followed by the seven year tribulation.

THE REVELATION OF JESUS CHRIST REVEALED

4. Followed by Jesus returning for the 1000-year reign during the millennium.

5. Afterward elimination of the curse and eternity with God for the redeemed.

Verse 11 This scripture is explaining to us that the eternal existence of man is determined while he is alive.

Hebrew 9:27, "And as it is appointed unto men once to die, but after this the judgment."

According to this scripture, we only die once followed by the judgment. This does not mean that the judgment will be immediate. We have already learned that those who accepted salvation through the sacrifice of Jesus Christ on the cross will not be judged to condemnation.

The word *once* in this scripture is very important while keeping in mind that no scripture contradicts another because all scriptures are the truth. There is no second chance to get it right following death no matter what a second chance is called.

There is no *purgatory*—an intermediate state after death for expiatory purification; (2) a place or state of temporary suffering or misery.

Neither is there no *reincarnation*—the idea or belief that people are born again with a different body after death, someone who has been born again with a different body after death, rebirth in new bodies or forms of life, especially a rebirth of a soul in a new human body; (2) a fresh embodiment.

Also, there is no *transmigration*—to cause to go from one state or existence or place to another; to pass at death from one body or being to another.

In the spirit of fairness, I just shared with you the definitions of *purgatory, reincarnation, and transmigration* as defined in the Merriam-Webster Dictionary.

If a person dies righteous at death, his soul and spirit go to heaven to await the resurrection of the body during the rapture and first resurrection (2 Corinthians 5:8–10, 1 Thessalonians 4:16–17).

If the person dies wicked, his soul and spirit go to hell to await the resurrection of his body (Revelation 20:13).

There is a saying that goes like this: If you are born twice (a natural and spiritual birth) you will die once; If you are born once (a natural birth only) you will die twice.

Verse 12 This verse is red lettered if you have a red-lettered edition bible this means Jesus is talking. The word quickly, in this case, means that Jesus could come at any time. If we are having church one Sunday morning or Wednesday night and the skies suddenly open up with the coming of Jesus Christ that would be quick. Jesus said the same thing in verse 7 that He would come quickly.

Remember the righteous will not be judged at the great white throne of judgment because we will have already been in heaven following the rapture, but we will be at the great white throne of judgment. The scripture says rewards to *every man* according to his work. There is no other way to interpret this except that every man will be rewarded according to his work.

1 Corinthians 3:12–15

Here, we are told that though the works may burn the man or woman shall be saved if Jesus Christ is their foundation. Some things people try to build upon a foundation of Jesus Christ are:

1. False doctrine

2. Conduct related to others (relationships)

3. Envying

4. Strife

5. Divisions

6. Bigotry

7. Personal ambition

8. Love of praise for self

9. Pride of denomination

10. Pride of talents

11. Love of authority (likely abusive when in charge)

These 11 things are just examples of what wood, hay, and stubble would look like to the Lord when handing out rewards. These things mentioned would burn up in the fire like wood, hay, or stubble (verse 12).

However, your love for God and man would not burn up in the fire. This love would be compared to gold, silver, and precious stones which will not burn up in fire (verse 12).

Revelation 22:13 Alpha is the first letter of the Greek alphabet and Omega is the last letter of the Greek alphabet. So when Jesus says here that He is: "Alpha and Omega, the beginning and the end, the first and the last," He is solidifying what is being said by saying it three different ways in one verse. In Revelations 1:17 and 2:8, it only Reads that Jesus is the *first and last*.

Verse 14 we are blessed when we follow the commandments of God, Reading the bible is not enough. Hearing the preacher is not enough. Instead., we must LIVE out the commandments of God.

There are approximately 1050 commands in the New Testament for Christians to obey. It is these commands that give Christians the overcoming lifestyle that we all seek in this life on earth.

Matthew 19:17, Matthew 22:36–40, John 14:15, John 14:21, John 15:10, 1 Corinthians 7:19, 1 John 2:3–5, 1 John 5:2–3, 2 John 6, Revelation 14:12.

1 John 3:22–24, Read

This is how you become the overcomer the Bible speaks of:

1. Believe on the name of Jesus for your salvation

2. Love one another, which is a commandment

3. Receiving the Holy Spirit by keeping the commandments

James 1:22–25, Read

Doing or living out the commandments of God will give us the right to eternal life and the right to enter into the gates of New Jerusalem. Remember in Revelation 21:12, there are 12 gates and an angel guarding each gate. The reason the angels are there is found in Revelation 21:27 to prevent *anything that defileth, neither whatsoever worketh abomination, or maketh a lie* from entering in through the gate.

Verse 15 We are told here again as in Revelation 21:8 that dogs, sorcerers, whoremongers, murderers, idolaters, and whosoever loveth and maketh a lie will not enter into eternal life nor will they enter into the New Jerusalem.

The terms *loveth a lie* and *maketh a lie* can be two different people. The lover of a lie can be the one who helps promote the liar by supporting a lie, like the gossiper. The maker of a lie can be the one who originates the lie, the teller.

I want to expound on the term *dogs* in verse 15 first by saying this is a reference to people and not animals. Dogs is a term used to describe false prophets and homosexuals in scripture:

Deuteronomy 23:18

Notice that the dog is used in conjunction with the word whore. We know that whore is usually referring to a woman. Here, the term dog is used to refer to a male prostitute, homosexual, or sodomite. This scripture is an instruction that they shall not use any money derived from such services as a contribution toward God.

Isaiah 56:10–11

Here, the term *dogs* are referring to false prophets. We know this because words like *blind watchmen* and *shepherds who cannot understand* are used to describe these people.

Philippians 3:2

We are told to beware of dogs. Here, the term *dogs* are referring to those who were putting more confidence in their flesh with the circumcision then with the sacrifice of Jesus

Christ on the cross. You will have to Read the scriptures that follow to understand this concept.

Philippians 3:18

To teach anything other than the saving power of the sacrifice and resurrection of our Lord and Savior Jesus Christ makes that person *an enemy of the cross.*

Verse 16 Keeping in mind that at this time all the battles have been fought and won. The Antichrist, the false prophet, and the dragon have been cast into the lake of fire and brimstone, the great white throne of judgment has occurred, we are beyond the 1000-year millennium and now have entered into eternal life.

Now, near the end of the book of Revelations, Jesus is saying

THE REVELATION OF JESUS CHRIST REVEALED

the same thing he said in Revelation 1:1, further authenticating this book with more than one witness.

That *I am* is significate. Remember what God told Moses his name was?

Exodus 3:14, Read

Remember what happened when Jesus identified himself when the soldiers came to arrest him.

John 18:5–6, Read

Revelation 5:5–7, Read

Verse 5 is identifying Jesus as the *Lion of the tribe of Judah* and *the Root of David*. The genealogy of Jesus can be found in Matthew 1.

Verse 6 There is the throne which means there is only one throne. We know from Revelation 5:1 that God the Father is sitting on the throne holding the book with the seven seals. Now, we are Reading here that *in the midst of the throne stood a Lamb as it had been slain.* We know this signifies Jesus who was slain for our sacrifice. Also, keep in mind that the 24 elders have their own seat around the throne, Revelation 4:4. Additionally, the four beasts are around the throne worshipping God, Revelation 4:8. Jesus is standing in this verse prior to taking the book.

Verse 7 The Lamb (Jesus) is identified as *He.* It is Jesus who took the book from the hand of Him, God the Father, *that sat on the throne.*

Acts 7:55–56

Stephen is in trouble here and when we Read the scriptures following we know that soon after Stephen saw inside heaven he was stoned to death. What I want to point out here is that Jesus is standing on behalf of Stephen. In Revelation 5:6, Jesus was standing when he took the book that no one else could open from the hand of God the Father.

I still believe that when I am in trouble, Jesus stands up for me also. In fact, with me believing this, because I stay in trouble quite a bit, Jesus probably stands for me more than He sits.

Revelation 22:17

The Holy Spirit and the bride are calling for all men to be saved. We understand the calling of the Holy Spirit because he is with us now. However, the calling of the bride is something probably better appreciated and understood by our Jewish brothers and sisters.

Old Testament prophets prophesied, in the scriptures, for centuries to the nation of Israel about the coming of a messiah to set his kingdom up here on earth. This does finally happen in Revelation Chapter 21.

We learned in Revelation 21:2 that the New Jerusalem is prepared by God the Father as a bride Adorned for her husband. Additionally, in Revelation 21:19–21, we Read about how the foundations of the New Jerusalem *were garnished with all manner of precious stones.*

In other words, both Jews and Gentiles are invited together to be with the Lord. The Holy Spirit and the bride *say come.*

Verse 18 This book is speaking of the book of Revelation because John is the writer of *this book.* The rest is self-explained. I pray that I have not been in error and Added nothing to the teaching of this book.

Verse 19 I believe that by the grace of God, I have taught you the truth about this book of prophecy.

The last part of verse 19 gives us three things that God shall do to anyone who subtracts from the words of this book. That word *shall* is a firm word. The three things are:

1. Remove his name from the book of life. We Read about this as a possibility in Exodus 32:32–33; Psalm 69:20–29; Revelation 3:5.

2. He will not be allowed into the Holy City. We Read about this possibility in Revelation 21:27.

3. He will not receive the blessings written in this book. We are told of the blessing in Revelation 1:3; Revelation 22:7.

Verse 20 Notice it is stated here, *surely, I come quickly.* I have the red-lettered edition which means this is something that Jesus said. Actually, this was said by Jesus in verse 12 but I believe it was Jesus actually talking in verse 12 because of what is said in verse 13. However, going back to

Revelation 22:20, we know Jesus said this but because of the way the verse began I believe it is John repeating what Jesus said.

Remember the red-lettered edition was man's idea not God's. The red letters are designed to serve as quotation marks of what Jesus said but it is possible that there may be places where Jesus spoke and the red letters are not there. John urges Jesus to come. This was approximately 2000 years ago.

The world is in disarray because just like in John's time they are being told today that Jesus is coming soon. Of course, there is no excuse for sin. There is a song I love titled "One by One." Now with that in mind knowing that we all don't die at the same time and knowing how we lie down in death is how we will rise at the rapture makes it clear to me that we should be more concerned with how we live this life instead of concerning ourselves with the timing of Jesus' return.

Verse 21 John is requesting that the unmerited favor of God, through Jesus Christ, be with us all.

The word *amen* means truly or truth and in Revelation 3:14 it is used as one of the titles of Jesus.

1 Corinthians 15:24–28

THE END OF TIME AND THE BEGINNING OF ETERNAL LIFE WITH GOD!!!

Made in the USA
Middletown, DE
09 February 2019